Granite Lake Wolves

Wolf Signs

Wolf Flight

Wolf Games

Wolf Tracks

Wolf Line

Wolf Nip

Takhini Wolves

Black Gold

Silver Mine

Diamond Dust

Moon Shine

Takhini Shifters

Copper King

Laird Wolf

A Lady's Heart

Wild Prince

A full list of Vivian's print titles is available on her website

www.vivianarend.com

PRAISE FOR VIVIAN AREND

"Vivian Arend does a wonderful job of building the atmosphere and the other characters in this story so that readers will be sucked into the world and looking forward to the rest of the books in the series."
~ *Library Journal*

"Steamy and sweet complete with a whole host of colourful side characters and enough sub-plots to get your teeth into. A fab read!"
~ *Scorching Book Reviews*

"There's a real chemistry between the characters, laced with humor and snappy dialogue and no shortage of steamy sex scenes to keep things lively. The result is an entertaining, spicy romance."
~ *Publishers Weekly*

Silver Mine is an outstanding story. The author creates a world that invites readers for the ride of their lives."
~ *Coffee Time Romance Reviews*

Arend offers constant action and thrills, and her characters are so captivating and nuanced that readers will have a hard time guessing who the villains really are.
~ *RT Book Reviews*

WOLF TRACKS

NORTHERN LIGHTS EDITION

VIVIAN AREND

This is a work of fiction. Names, characters, places, and incidents either are the product of the author's imagination or are used fictitiously, and any resemblance to any persons, living or dead, business establishments, events, or locales is entirely coincidental.

This one's for you—the readers. From Molli, who's been begging for TJ's story since day one, to the woman who emailed to tell me she read the whole series back to back over a weekend. You are why this story was even written. Thank you for taking the wolfies and giving them so much loving.

Arwhooooo.

1

*P*am let out a long, slow whistle and stared out the window to admire the scenery one more time. "Damn it, Maggie, I knew you were hiding something, but seriously. How many can I take home?"

A light tap on her arm dragged her attention away from the backyard and the succulent array of man flesh congregating there. "You're supposed to be helping me, not drooling over the wedding guests." Maggie turned her back and gestured over her shoulder. "Get the last of my buttons, will you?"

"Where did you get this gorgeous gown so quickly up here in the boonies? I mean, it's been two months since you went north. Not that I've been calculating or anything, but sixty-seven days is a short time to fall in love, get engaged and arrange to tie the knot." Pam slipped the last of the minuscule pearl buttons through the hoops. Two months since she'd seen her friend, and falling in love didn't seem to be the only thing that had changed. Pam checked the bedroom they were in with a growing suspicion Maggie was keeping secrets from her. Something wasn't sitting right, and over the years Pam had learned to trust her instincts.

"It's my sister's dress. I just had to add a little bit of lace to the bottom to deal with the difference in our heights." Maggie twirled, the lacey layers of the skirt flying around her. Her short blonde hair bounced more wildly than usual, a thin silver tiara nestled amidst the shimmer. "How do I look?"

Pam rolled her eyes. "Like a freaking pixie queen, as usual. God, why do you even ask? You'd be gorgeous in a paper bag."

Maggie laughed.

It was now or never. "I need to know, Mags. Is this really something you want to do? Or are you getting married this fast because, oh, you feel you have to…"

Her best friend frowned. "Do you think I'm being forced into this? Seriously, I'm in love and I want to marry Erik."

"You're not pregnant and thinking this is the only way to deal with it, 'cause, if you are, I'd be totally fine with helping support you—"

"Pam!" Maggie trapped her in her arms, squeezed with the tightest bear hug possible. "Oh, sweetie, I'm honoured you're willing to help me, but I'm not pregnant. I'm honestly and truly in love. I know it seems fast, but with some…people, you know it's right."

That was possible. Maybe. Pam had rarely seen it. She turned away to stop Maggie from reading her expression too closely. Just because she'd never seen a real-life "love you forever" didn't mean it couldn't happen, and someone's wedding day was hardly the time to point that out.

She sighed and tried to distract herself with the man candy again. "So. When you and Erik take off on your honeymoon, do I get to sample the locals?"

Maggie's laugh tickled her ears and then everything was okay again. "You're such a flirt. Go easy on them, heartbreaker. Hey, I need a few minutes alone. Why don't you go explore? Come back in about twenty and I'll be ready to roll."

Pam kissed her cheek. "If you're sure you're sure."

"God, go on. I'm a big girl now." They grinned at each other with the familiarity of long-time friends before Pam scooted downstairs. She peeked into the bustling kitchen before wandering out into the yard.

"Hey, can I get you a drink?"

"Are you hungry?"

Suddenly surrounded by tall men in formal suits, her mouth watered. Another voice lifted over the others and a light touch landed on her shoulder.

"Here. For you." A Gerard Butler look-alike offered her a glass of white wine. She shook her head. Did they think she just fell off the turnip truck? She didn't take drinks from strange men, even drool-worthy ones.

"You're Maggie's friend, right?"

"Would you like to go for a walk for a few minutes? I can show you around the yard."

One of them offered his elbow and she batted her lashes as she took it. Why not? She had time before Maggie wanted her back. A couple of children raced past their feet and Pam smiled as she watched the happy chaos filling the festively decorated yard. "Nice crowd for the wedding. Do all you boys live around here?"

It had been awhile since she'd had such tasty company, let alone this many good-looking guys. While the attention was diverting, she wasn't in the market for a relationship while she was in the North. Nope. She'd do the "support my friend" thing with Maggie, take off for a little sightseeing, then it was back to civilization all the way. And beautiful men like these—well, a one-night stand would be fun, but the bridesmaid getting it on at the wedding was a cliché she really wanted to avoid in this lifetime.

Maggie's fiancé strode over, towering above the other men.

Pam chuckled. While he'd turned out to be one of the good guys, she'd still kick his butt if he needed it, no matter how big he was. No one messed with her friends, and Maggie was her oldest friend. BFF and all that shit.

"You doing okay? The boys treating you right?" Erik glanced around, his expression stern, and the fawning crew raced away like they'd been shot out of a cannon.

Pam stared at their retreating backs with growing suspicion. No way. If he'd put them up to it...

"I guess that's the question, isn't it?" She narrowed her eyes. "I was getting the royal treatment. That your doing?"

Erik held up his hands, palms out. "Trust me. I don't feel like having you tear a strip off me. If they're hanging around, it's because you're interesting. Just don't break too many hearts, okay? I'd hate to have to listen to sucky love songs during karaoke night for months after you leave."

Pam laughed. "Okay, you're safe. I believe you." She shook her head as she glanced up and down his length. "What the hell do you guys eat up here? Is there like a fountain of hugeness or something? I've counted at least two dozen men over six-three in height."

He grinned. "It's the water. Seriously good. Hey, Maggie says she needs you one last time, but I was hoping to introduce you to my best man first." He glanced around. "Only he seems to have disappeared."

Pam waved a hand. "I'll meet him when we do the little walk-thing around the yard. Maggie explained the procedure, and I'm cool with the ceremony. I'd better run and see what she wants. Just in case she's getting cold feet and wants me to call the whole thing off on her behalf."

She hid her amusement as his smile drained away. "You don't think she would? But..."

It had taken years to perfect the fake concerned expression she wore as she nodded sympathetically at him. "I'm sure it will be fine, but I'd better go settle her down. You stay here and try not to worry." She patted him on the arm and went back upstairs, snickering evilly.

Maggie met her at the top of the landing. Pam tried to wipe her face clean of her grin, but they'd been best friends for too long.

"Who are you tormenting now? Pam, you promised not to freak people out with your weird sense of humour."

Someone stepped to the side of Maggie. Pam turned to face the young man and stopped dead.

My oh my.

She flushed at the expression in his eyes. The last time a guy had stared at her like that, the two of them had been naked, in the middle of a heated sexual exchange. He stripped her with his gaze and rather than feel indignant, her own interest rose. Of course, he was too young for her, but still...

Hot damn, he *was* hot. Darkish skin, black hair. Eyes so black the pupils and irises bled together. That must be it—his pupils—it only looked like he was one step away from ravishing her.

"Pam, I'd like you to meet TJ. He's a good friend and works with Erik as a wilderness guide. He's going to be our best man."

TJ held out his hand, stepping closer, and she forced herself to resist backing away.

She grasped his fingers, intending to give him a firm business-like handshake when he flipped her palm down and raised her hand to his mouth. "My pleasure. Really."

He leaned forward and kissed her knuckles.

An icy chill slipped up her spine, and oh my word, her body grew instantly wet. *Damn!* Did he just lick her skin?

She knew she was staring, but there seemed to be no way to tear her gaze from his. Even after he straightened, he refused to let her fingers drop and she stood there like some freaking garden gnome statue with her hand limp-wristed in his, hoping by some weird circumstance they'd magically turn out to be standing alone in a bedroom with a mattress on the firm side bumping the back of her knees.

Lust stole her tongue.

"TJ?" Maggie elbowed him and he shook himself, like he was waking up.

He took a deep breath and his eyes widened even farther.

Pam glanced away, anywhere had to be safer than staring into those fuck-me-now bedroom eyes. Until she noticed she'd lowered her gaze and watched the front of his dress pants tent, his erection growing more and more obvious.

"Pam?" She dragged her gaze up to see Maggie examining her with concern. "I think we need to go downstairs. Right now."

Maggie tugged her arm, pulling her toward the top of the stairs and away from the fascinating young man in the tuxedo.

With a deep sense of regret, Pam turned her back on the dark god who watched her with hungry eyes.

Shit.

Shit.

TJ swallowed hard and immediately regretted it. His tongue had picked up the flavour of the woman Maggie had dragged off, and now the chemicals once again raced through his body, making him ache.

Shit.

How was it possible? Maggie had pulled him aside to warn him, *again*, he couldn't let her friend know anything about them being wolves because Pam was full human. He was not to let the werewolf out of the bag, so to speak.

He felt a little indignant Maggie treated him like a child and expected him to screw up. Just because he'd accidentally shifted once before. Or twice.

But both those instances were years ago. He was twenty-two, and while he still preferred his wolf form for high-dexterity moves, his human was getting better. Besides, Keil had already issued orders in his high and mighty Alpha voice for all pack members to remain unfurry for the duration of the wedding. No one would disobey his direct command.

Still...*shit*.

It was a good thing Maggie *had* warned him, because incredibly his first impulse upon laying eyes on the beauty was to shift and bury his nose in her dark brown hair. He wanted to sniff her all over, then change back to human form to lick her, starting at her toes and getting delightfully distracted long before reaching anywhere near her throat.

His cock ached, and his vision blurred. Damn if his hearing wasn't buzzing as well.

Suddenly the world began to shake and he wondered how badly he'd lost it before he realized Erik had grabbed him by the arms and stared into his face with concern.

"TJ? What the hell is up? Maggie called me through our mental link and told me to get up here and deal with you. Were you about to shift?"

That settled TJ quickly.

"No!" Crap, not another doubter of his ability to hold it together. Although something was seriously screwed up. He sighed. "It's just…"

He closed his eyes and took a deep sniff. Erik's scent was the strongest, followed by Maggie's, but wrapping around them both was a tantalizing and intoxicating aroma that tickled his libido and kicked it into overdrive. "Erik, are we *sure* Pam doesn't have wolf in her bloodline?"

Erik leaned back and crossed his arms. "Positive. Maggie lived with her for years. Both the Omegas have met her, and she's pure human. One hundred percent." His gaze narrowed. "What are you not saying?"

TJ wrinkled his nose. "You know how you've always said I've got a keen sense of smell?"

"The best in the pack."

He snorted and shook his head. "Then you'll be pleased to know my awesome sniffer has just told me Maggie's best friend, fully human and not possibly eligible for the honour…is my damn mate."

2

―――――

He'd found a new form of hell. TJ paced slowly around the outer edge of the backyard, his freaking mate on his arm, and all he could talk about was…nothing.

He couldn't tell her he was weak at the knees at the thought of finding her. Couldn't say how important she was to him. He concentrated on keeping his feet on the ground because there was no way he was going to trip and be an ass in front of her.

Erik had made him swear he wouldn't say anything prematurely. Until TJ talked to his brother, the Alpha, chatting up his mate was outlawed, and the kicker was Erik had actually pulled a Beta move and *ordered* TJ to stay quiet. The damn hierarchy of the pack froze his tongue.

Now torn between the dire need to haul Pam off somewhere private to bind them together for the rest of their days and the violent need to obey a direct command— TJ was screwed.

He glanced sideways to admire her again. A few dark strands had fallen from the fancy hairdo framing her face. She smiled at everyone, but the tension in her body screamed at him, and all he wanted to do was ease her burden.

"You okay?"

She met his gaze then flushed darker. "How many times do we do this?"

"Walk the loop? Three. You should slow down a bit so we don't step on Erik's and Maggie's heels." He pulled his elbow in so the back of her fingers touched his ribs. True, there were a few layers of clothing between them, but it was better than nothing.

This was driving him mad. He smelled her skin, the natural perfume of her body.

Her arousal.

His heart pounded, and he strove to keep his face neutral and not pant like a dog. How everyone around didn't notice they were both drenched in mating scents was beyond his comprehension.

Another deep breath made his mouth water and his cock jerk. There was no denying it. It was nearly impossible but it had happened. His one-and-only forever mate was a human.

He was okay with it. It was weird and insane, but since they were mates, there was a reason for it, and they'd figure it out. First it seemed he was going to have to not only convince her they belonged together, but the entire leadership of his pack.

Starting with big brother Keil and his mate Robyn. The Alphas of the Granite Lake pack sat in the front row with their little girl perched quietly on Keil's knee.

Robyn frowned at TJ, using sign language to unobtrusively ask what was wrong. He shook his head quickly. This wasn't going to be an easy explanation.

Pam unconsciously rubbed her fingers up and down his arm. The slight movement taunted him. Drove him insane.

He reached over and placed his other hand on top of hers. "Don't."

She stiffened in response and tried to pull away.

Pain raced through him at having his mate unsure and a little frightened, and suddenly he didn't give a *damn* what his Beta had told him. His tongue loosened, the restriction binding him falling away. He was going to care for her, let her know everything was going to be okay. If he happened to mention he wanted her sometime during the conversation...so be it.

He leaned his head closer, breathing in as much of her scent as possible. "It's okay. You were tickling me. I like you holding me, but the rubbing was distracting."

She stayed silent for a moment then adjusted her grip. "I'm sorry. I didn't mean to."

TJ laughed softly. "You're distracting no matter what you're doing." He smiled at her and winked. "I kinda like it."

She frowned. "Like what?"

"Being distracted by you."

She shook her head as they took the corner at the far end of the yard and headed back to the starting position for the second lap. "How old are you?"

He paused. "Why?"

In spite of licking her lips and sending a shot of lust through his core, the expression in her eyes was friendly, not flirtatious. "I don't rob cradles."

Damn it. "I'm legal in all states and provinces."

"You're a baby. Cute, but a baby."

"Is that why you wanted to crawl into bed with me when we met at the top of the stairs?" She stumbled, and he caught her quickly. "Shit. Sorry, that wasn't very polite. True, but not very polite."

"I did not want to—"

"Careful. Maggie told me you were the most honest and trustworthy person she'd ever met. Hate to ruin your reputation."

She growled and he grinned. Feisty wench. He liked that in a woman.

"Fine. You're a good-looking guy and yeah, I did picture tangling the sheets with you." *Hallelujah!* "But you're too young. I'm here for the wedding and that's it."

TJ tried to keep the image of them naked in bed from distracting him as they walked in silence for another few paces. Unfortunately he had a good imagination.

The too-young thing he could work around. The fact she was being stubborn? Oh, he loved a challenge.

"Stop it," she whispered. Her voice was deep and husky, slipping like a caress over his already super-sensitive nerves.

"Stop what?"

She wiggled her hand on his arm. "That. You're...rubbing me."

Oops. He stilled his thumb from the circles he was tracing on the back of her hand. Seemed neither of them could resist touching each other, which only made sense as mates.

A faint flush covered her soft skin from the low neckline of her dress up to her hairline, and he had to look away before he did something too wolfish like drop her to the ground and lick her until she screamed in pleasure.

"What happens after the ceremony?" Pam asked. "I forgot to check with Maggie to see if there was anything I needed to do."

I take you home and make love to you all night long. "We head in, enjoy dinner, then I'm singing before the dance begins."

"You sing?" There was a trace of something in her voice. Doubt?

"I sing. Are you surprised?"

"Not at all," she lied.

TJ snorted. It was a deception he recognized easily. After too many years of being expected to screw things up, he knew exactly what someone meant when they spoke in that particular tone of voice.

"You want to join me for a few songs?" he teased.

She choked for a second. "Trust me, that would be a bad idea. In fact, for a wedding gift I'm considering swearing to Maggie to never attempt to sing in her presence again."

"That bad, huh?"

"Put it this way, I can hit notes they haven't invented yet."

He chuckled and she joined him in laughing, and suddenly the wall she'd wedged between them crumbled a little.

They paced slowly, following Maggie and Erik on the final circle of the yard.

"So if you won't sing, will you dance with me?" Surely he could keep his feet under him for long enough to dance without making a fool of himself. Of them both.

The grip she had on his arm tightened slightly. "I'll consider it. Looks like there's a lot of single guys around to choose from."

Do not growl. Do not *growl.*

It took all his strength to fight the instant urge to claim her in front of the whole damn pack. Like *hell* was she going to dance with anyone other than him. "I get first dance though, you know, wedding party and all."

"That might be...nice."

Nice? Bloody hell.

He ignored the questioning glances his big brother shot in his direction.

Fine, maybe Pam didn't know about werewolves, and maybe he was in for a hell of a lot of trouble figuring out how he was going to solve this mess, but one thing he knew without a doubt.

She was going to be his. Body and soul.

TJ stepped around her, positioning her at Maggie's right hand. Pam shivered as he leaned in close and brushed his lips lightly against the skin beside her ear.

He spoke barely above a whisper. "I guarantee it's going to be a whole lot more memorable than *nice*."

PAM STOOD TO THE SIDE, her fingers squeezing so hard around the flower arrangement Maggie had passed her she heard some of the flower stems crack.

Across from her, TJ held her gaze with his and damn, the man was enough to distract a saint. She barely heard Erik and Maggie exchange vows, she was too caught up in admiring his clean-cut good looks. Getting lost in his mesmerizing dark eyes. She wanted to interrupt the ceremony to demand he stare elsewhere, but at the same time she couldn't help but be flattered.

Maybe a short fling wouldn't be such a bad idea after all.

The whole service passed in a blur as they locked eyes. Inside, a flame burned, desire wrapped around her core and made her heart pound. There had to be something in the northern air causing her to react like a sex-crazed ninny.

A discreet cough brought her back to her senses, and she hurried to join Maggie and Erik as they moved down the aisle between the chairs, headed for the hall.

TJ's warm hand slid around her waist and goose bumps rose. He ignored her wiggled attempt to dislodge him, instead tucking her tightly against his side and lowering his head until his lips hovered an inch over her ear. She waited for him to whisper something wicked, something in keeping with the heat of passion he'd been throwing at her for the past umpteen minutes.

The anticipation was killing her, and she swore her panties were wet just thinking about him saying something sexy.

"Chicken?"

Not sexy. "What?"

"Or fish? What do you want for dinner?"

She laughed out loud and relaxed against him. "You're a goof."

TJ sighed mightily. "So I've been told."

For the next hour he proceeded to enchant her, anticipating her every need. They sat to one side of the bridal couple, and throughout the meal he touched her constantly.

"You treat all your visitors like this?" she asked. Blood pounded through her hard enough she could have just finished a marathon.

TJ topped up the wine in her glass as he shook his head.

"I can honestly say you're the first woman I've ever treated this way." He rested his arm on the back of her chair and her nipples tightened.

Would anyone notice if she crawled into his lap and sucked face with him for a while?

Someone at the end of the hall tinkled their wine glass, and the entire room joined in. Maggie and Erik rose good-naturedly and when he dipped her, kissing her passionately, the crowd shouted their approval. The whole event was exactly the kind of celebration Pam had hoped her best friend would experience.

TJ squeezed her shoulder as he stood and made his way to the front. He grabbed an acoustic guitar from somewhere and plopped himself on a stool.

A murmur rose from the crowd, and TJ grinned sheepishly.

"Yeah, it's a new guitar, but this time it's not my fault. A certain little boy I was babysitting thought the old one would make a dandy boat."

Gentle laughter carried through the air as TJ tuned the strings, his fingers moving smoothly. He turned to address Erik and Maggie. "I know you requested your favourites, but if you'd humour me, I have a song I wrote a while back. I've been saving it for a special moment, and I think this is about as special as it can get. It's called 'Eternal Love'."

He strummed a few chords before slipping into a simple melody, fingers picking individual notes to accompany his rich tenor. Their gazes met, and he sang to her.

Pam's throat tightened. She shifted uncomfortably in her chair as she listened to the lyrics. It was all so airy-fairy and impossible and yet—something deep inside wished it was possible for a love like he sang about to be real.

A love that lasted forever? Fresh each morning?

Bullshit.

Pretty sad thoughts to be entertaining while at a wedding.

She dragged her gaze off TJ to where Maggie and Erik sat staring into each other's eyes. For what it was worth, she wished them the best. Maggie deserved to be happy, and hopefully Erik was the guy to make it happen.

Well, he'd damn well better or she'd rip him a new one for hurting her best friend.

Pam sighed and leaned back in her chair. She closed her eyes and let the music swirl around her. TJ's mellow voice touched her in places she didn't want to think about. Places she'd closed the door on, and she'd never been one to linger over the past.

Nope, get over it and go on—that was her motto. Life was for living to the max, enjoying every experience as much as possible. One day at a time.

She sat straighter and resolutely faced the singer who made her belly quiver with each new note he sang. TJ's fingers caressed the strings, and she pictured him touching her with that same intensity, same attention to detail, and the pulse between her legs kicked into high gear again.

Holy Toledo, she was getting turned on watching the guy play his guitar.

What the heck had she been drinking? There was something going on, the way her gaze kept being drawn back to TJ, the way his voice tickled in her ears and made her skin burn. The urge to go for a little tumble while she was here increased. Maggie wouldn't mind.

Besides, it wasn't like she was leaving in the morning. She had her adventure trip scheduled to start in a couple days.

A few nights' excitement could be what she needed to make this a very memorable holiday.

He sang the final notes and let the tune fade away.

The rest of the guests clapped and whistled in appreciation. TJ finally broke eye contact with her and smiled out at the crowd, before motioning for a few others to join him. They picked up instruments, and the group lit into a lively tune. Chairs and tables were dragged aside, and the hall became a bustling hive of noise as everyone stepped in to rearrange and make space for dancing.

Pam moved a couple chairs before realizing she was more of a hindrance than help. She snuck to the side and watched in fascination as the room transformed before her eyes.

Up on the stage, TJ and another guitarist strummed something with a hard-rock beat, and the rhythm pulsed in time with her heart. His dark hair shone in the light as he rocked, and she wondered if it would feel fine or coarse if she ran her fingers through it.

"Did you enjoy that?" Maggie asked.

Pam jumped a little, then let out the breath she'd been holding. "Hey. Fabulous ceremony, and the meal was delicious."

Her friend nodded in agreement. "It was good, but I meant the singing. I didn't expect TJ to share a song he'd written himself. It was beautiful."

"He's got a great voice," Pam admitted. Maggie smiled past her and Pam glanced over her shoulder to see Erik hanging back. "You guys taking off soon?"

Her friend nodded. "I wanted to make sure everything was kosher with you. We'll be back tomorrow afternoon, and have some more time to visit before you take off on your excursion and we leave on our honeymoon." She wrinkled her nose. "You going to be okay with us leaving you? Because I could—"

Pam slapped a hand over her friend's mouth for a second. "Oh no, girlfriend. You weren't about to suggest you'd stick around on your wedding night to babysit me, were you?"

"Hell, no." Maggie grinned. "I was going to say if you wanted to you could go home early and hide. I've got all your favourite videos, and there's microwave popcorn in the cupboard."

Pam deliberately glanced around, eyeing the smartly dressed men before turning to smirk at Maggie. "You think I want to go watch *Serenity* for the millionth time when you've got this kind of a smorgasbord laid out for me?"

"They are kind of tasty, aren't they?" Maggie turned, and they both gazed into the room.

It was a little annoying that the first place her gaze went was to where TJ stood. *Shoot.*

Pam ignored the blatant interest running on a constant loop in her brain and grinned evilly. "Oh yeah, and there's one in particular who's been making me drool all afternoon."

"Really?" Maggie leaned closer and whispered. "Who?"

"That one." Pam pointed at Erik, laughing out loud when Maggie elbowed her.

"Hands off, sugar, get your own Friendly Giant."

The music started again, a slow tempo this time, and Maggie pulled Pam in for a hug. "Time for the first dance, then Erik and I are going to sneak away. I'll see you at dinner tomorrow, okay?"

Pam kissed her cheek quickly. "Don't worry about me. It's not like you're throwing me to the dogs."

Maggie snorted loudly. "At least you know how to handle them."

"Trust me, I can handle the two-legged variety as well as I deal with the four-legged. Now go on, your big brute is waiting, and even though I still think I could take him down, I'm going to be nice and not hurt him before you get to enjoy tonight."

Erik held out his hand. Maggie joined him with a laugh and the two of them spun off onto the dance floor.

Pam let out a long, slow breath. It was clear they were very much in love. Maybe it would work out. The lights of the hall dimmed, and a disco ball turned on. Pam fought back a snicker as sparkles danced over the walls and the lone pair in the spotlight.

Someone stepped in behind her, the heat of his solid body hitting her back as he wrapped his hands around her waist and gently nestled them together.

TJ.

Cocky bastard, really. She debated slamming a heel on his instep, or flipping him over her shoulder, just to teach him a lesson, but watching Maggie and Erik float around the floor had mellowed her too much.

"You should be careful putting the moves on a girl like that. You might lose something important," she warned.

He ignored the threat and rested his chin on her shoulder. The heat radiating between them tempted her. "They fit awesome together, don't they?"

His breath brushed her cheek, warm and sweet smelling. Her mouth watered, but she didn't want to talk romance with him.

"They look...unbalanced. What was Maggie thinking getting involved with someone so much taller than her?"

He *hmmed*. "They were probably thinking that when it's right, there's no denying you've found the one you want."

Oh lordy, his thumbs stroked her waist, and he nuzzled under her ear. Did she want this? Heat flushed her. She had to decide, and quick. She could lead him out onto the dance floor and enjoy his touch in public, or they could find a dark corner and see what else came up.

So to speak.

He tugged her backward, and her body overruled her mind. They slipped into the shadows at the side of the hall, ducking behind a room divider.

He pressed her against it, his solid body very, very warm. Her heart rate increased, as did the tingling sensation between her thighs, and she squeezed her legs together to stop the ache.

Man-oh-man, his eyes were so incredible she swore he was using some kind of hypnosis. Turning away was impossible as he stared at her, tracing her hair, her face, one finger outlining her lips before he slowly lowered his head and brought their mouths together.

He brushed his lips over hers like a gentle breeze, his fingers tugging her hair to redirect the angle of her head until their mouths meshed together. Tentative strokes of his tongue moved fleetingly past her teeth. Teasing, barely giving her a taste of him before he broke away and dropped his forehead against hers.

"Holy shit, you taste good," he panted. "Incredibly fabulous. I'd never dreamed a woman could taste like you. Or make me feel the way you make me feel."

Screw the sweet talk. She hadn't had nearly enough of his kisses. She tried to regain possession of his lips. Arched her back in an attempt to press their bodies together and let her feel his muscles, his desire for her.

He groaned softly. "You're killing me. We shouldn't…"

She stepped on either side of his leg and pasted her aching crotch to his thigh. A short gasp escaped her as the impact made her clit throb.

"Fuck it." TJ grabbed her butt and dragged her hard against him, wrestling control from her as this time he kissed her senseless. Sucked the air from her lungs, twined their tongues together. An almost desperate, mindless, seeking touch. He demanded her response, and she gave it eagerly. The pleasure in her sex rose like a rocket blasting into outer space.

His hands were everywhere. Skimming her torso, touching her breasts. Clutching her hips and grinding her hard onto his thigh. Excitement washed over her, the rapid beat of her pulse making her lightheaded, out of breath.

He licked a path down her neck, nibbled on her collarbone and something electric shot to her core.

"I want you, Pam," he growled against her skin. "You're going to be mine."

Sheesh, that comment pushed a few wrong buttons, but right here, right now? She wasn't about to argue with his macho-sexist statement as long as he kept doing what he was doing.

Lost beyond all reason, she teetered on the edge of an orgasm and if he stopped she would kill him. Pam clasped his head in her hands and hauled his mouth to hers as she leaned back and tried to find the final touch she needed to go over the edge.

The barrier at her back wobbled for a second, then tilted to the north. All their weight went with the wall as it tipped, crashing to the floor with them on top. She smothered her curses as the flames of desire building between them evaporated into thin air.

TJ's heavy breathing echoed in her ear as they unwound tangled limbs. The damn disco lights flickered over them, showcasing their undignified situation. Partygoers congregated to stare with concern and offer helping hands. Pam scrambled to her feet, but all she could think about was the aching need in her core, and the sweet taste of him lingering in her mouth.

3

$\mathcal{K}$eil pinched the bridge of his nose. TJ attempted to stand in one place and not fidget like a naughty school kid hauled in front of the principal.

"She's your mate."

"Screw it, Keil, I've told you a dozen times. If all you're going to do is repeat 'she's your mate' in a tone of voice suggesting I'm more than slightly brain-dead, we're hardly going to get anywhere with this conversation, are we?"

Robyn laughed.

"It's not funny," Keil complained.

Robyn tugged his arm and cupped her mate's face in her hands, staring into his eyes.

TJ watched as his brother and sister-in-law discussed him. He knew they were doing it, that talking-between-themselves thing mates could do.

He sighed. Well, most mates. He doubted he and Pam would be able to, since she wasn't wolf. Still, he wasn't going to argue with fate.

She was most definitely the one. Kissing the woman had been better than any sexual experience he'd had before in his life. He'd been rapidly approaching the point where he would have embarrassed himself and come in his pants. Then he'd managed, again, to muck things up.

So now he waited to be disciplined like a disobedient puppy by his Alpha pair.

What he wanted to do was figure out a way to find Pam and finish what they'd started. If she'd even speak to him after being rescued from the tangled mess they'd ended up in on the floor. Thankfully the lights had been dim enough everyone thought it was nothing more than his usual clumsy self, and not the two of them fooling around, that caused the accident.

A tug on his sleeve brought him back from his mental wanderings. Robyn smiled at him and used American Sign Language to talk to him. She signed slowly—he had learned a lot, but still wasn't fluent.

"If Pam is your mate, how are you going to deal with it?"

TJ hesitated. "You mean, like will I tell her about being a wolf?"

Robyn nodded.

Shoot, he hadn't thought about that. Hell if he knew. He tapped his right fingertips against his forehead several times then flung his hand to the right, ending with his palm out and all five fingers raised.

Robyn blew out a long, slow breath. "You don't know. So if we suggest you proceed slowly until you have figured it out, would that make sense?"

Fuck. "Why do you have to be so logical?" he complained.

"Would you prefer we ordered you to stay away from her until she leaves Alaska?" his brother asked.

Keil came and stood next to Robyn, the two of them together an immovable wall.

"She's my mate. You wouldn't be so cruel." *Would they?*

"We're not trying to hurt you, but we have to figure out the best thing for the entire pack. If she is your mate, and I'm not denying it, it's going to make things bloody awkward around here." Keil crossed his arms and leaned back on the table. "We've finally got the pack to the point they aren't complaining about full-blood and half-blood issues nearly so much, and now this?"

TJ ran a hand through his hair in frustration. "I didn't do it on purpose."

"No, but it's potentially pretty volatile to have a full human enter the mix."

"I'm not giving her up."

Robyn shook her head. She pushed Keil until he moved his bulk away with a sigh. "Fine, you talk to him. I'm going back to the party to make sure none of the pack gets into too much shit."

Keil kissed Robyn before he left—a sweet and tender kiss—and TJ's throat tightened with something between happiness and envy.

He'd always wanted to have a mate. To have someone to care for and enjoy their company, like he'd witnessed between his older brother and his wife. And now? It was potentially within his grasp.

Robyn settled on the couch. She checked him over carefully, and TJ's skin crawled.

"If you're planning on using your Super Alpha Powers of Obedience on me, I want to say upfront—that would totally suck."

She laughed as she lifted her hands to sign at him. "Keil tries so hard to be fair to the pack he forgets to be fair to you. No Alpha shit, just one question."

He sat across from her. In the past two and a half years since Robyn had joined the pack, she'd come a long way from being clueless about werewolves. Being deaf didn't stop her from being one of the most powerful—and creative —leaders he'd ever known. Maybe she had an idea of how he should deal with the mess.

"One question?"

"You don't know if she wants you…"

Well, if the little episode in the hall meant anything.

"…for anything other than a fling." Robyn stared expectantly.

Damn. "She's my—"

"Mate. I know, but she's not a wolf. You want her, and will always want her, but I don't think it works the same with humans, does it?"

TJ shrugged. "Never thought about it. I mean, I know there are wolves and humans who are married, but most of them are outcast wolves, who live packless..."

His stomach fell. If he took Pam as a mate, would they expect him to leave?

Granite Lake had always been his home, and while his mate was of vital importance, he didn't want to give up his pack. His family.

He dropped his head into his hands. Suddenly what should have been the most fabulous day of his life turned grey and cold.

Robyn touched his shoulder gently to get his attention. "We will never kick you out. If Pam is your mate, she's part of our family too, no matter what."

She stared at him for a little while, and a nervous twitch started in his thigh. He jiggled his legs to try and hide his reaction. This was a lot more complicated than he'd ever expected it to be.

Inside, his wolf fidgeted. It couldn't understand why they were sitting here instead of sniffing out the delicious-smelling female who belonged to them.

"You need to give her time. If she accepts you as a human, you'll have a better chance of her accepting you as a wolf. You can't go off half-cocked on this one, TJ. Take the time, do it right and make it last."

TJ snorted in derision. "How?"

"She's registered for the next expedition with Keil's wilderness excursion company. You're going along as a guide. Give her a chance to get to know you a little better in a setting you're comfortable in. See what happens, more than just physical attraction. But you must control your wolf."

He and Keil had already been preparing for the next wilderness trip. There was a group of ten signed up, including Pam. While he appreciated Robyn had a point, having to court his mate around a large group of people was stupid. There might be safety in numbers and everything, but he didn't want to have numbers. One plus one would be fine, thank you very much.

An idea rumbled in the back of his mind, and he tried very hard not to let anything show on his face. An excursion? Some time alone?

Oh yeah.

Loud clapping shook him from his reverie. Robyn lowered her hands and glared at him.

He leapt to his feet. "Sure, sounds great. Awesome idea, you know, taking some time to get to know her. You're a genius. Gorgeous, and a genius. What did Keil ever do without you?" *Babbling.* He was officially babbling.

How fast could he get out of the room before she figured out something was amiss?

He flashed her two thumbs up and dodged a footrest, aiming for the front door. "Well, gotta run. Lots to do in the next couple of days. Gotta get lots of sleep and keep my head and stay in control, right?"

He ducked outside before she could say anything like "What the hell are you planning and I forbid you to even think about pulling a fast one." Because what he had in mind was definitely on the not-going-to-be-approved list.

But this was his *mate* they were talking about here. As if Keil had waited longer than a day to claim Robyn.

TJ headed back toward the hall, a brisk five-minute walk up the gravel road from his Alpha's house. The music of the party carried through the air, and he hurried as fast as possible. The thought of finding Pam dancing with any of the other guys made the hair at the back of his neck stand upright. Oh no, waiting was out of the question.

He pulled out his cell phone and made the first call. "Hey, Jared? Get your ass off the dance floor for five minutes. I need to talk to you."

PAM THREW herself on the couch in Maggie's living room and groaned in frustration. Off in the distance she still heard dance music, but she'd lost interest after getting tossed to the ground like a piece of confetti.

Well, not true.

She'd brushed herself off, thankful for the dim lighting so no one saw how flushed her cheeks were. Still, accidents happen, and she'd been more than happy to head out onto the dance floor when the man of the moment had disappeared.

Great. So much for *forever*—the guy couldn't even stick around for long enough to finish giving her an orgasm.

She clicked on the TV and flicked through channels listlessly.

Maggie was gone with her true love, sexing it up wherever their bridal suite was. Pam had the run of the house, and all she could think about was how lonely it was going to be to crawl into bed tonight.

Gack. Horny and morose, what an insipid combination. She was well on the way to hitting all the high notes for a pity party in under an hour.

The door to the kitchen creaked, moving an inch, and she sat up to stare at it.

She hadn't heard anyone come in, but what with all the fun she was having watching *The Price is Right*, there could have been a dozen people in the next room.

"Hello?"

The door shifted again, and this time a silver-grey muzzle appeared, poking through the crack.

Pam frowned. She didn't know Maggie and Erik had a dog. She knelt on the seat cushion and watched more carefully. The animal took a few cautious sniffs, its nostrils flaring.

"Hey, what're you doing?" All the signs were there for her to read—classic nonaggressive behavior, curiosity more than anything. Pam smiled. "Come on, don't be afraid."

Even though the beast didn't act hostile, once its full head popped through the doorway, Pam swore.

"Holy shit, no one told me they kept wolves as pets here. Good...wolfie. *Stay.*"

The silver-grey creature had made it into the room, sitting obediently at her command. Pam blew out a slow breath of air. Thank God for well-trained animals.

She came around the couch cautiously to examine the wolf.

It seemed to be staring back just as intently, panting softly, its tongue lolling to one side.

She held out a hand and allowed herself to be sniffed. "So, I've got a buddy for tonight. You tired of dancing as well? Going to hang with me for a girl's night out?"

The wolf snorted, a gust of air rushing past her hand. Pam touched the animal's muzzle gently, brushing the coarse fur, rubbing its ears.

"There you go. It's okay. I'm not going to hurt you."

What a beautiful creature. She wasn't sure what other lineage had been crossbred with the wolf, but the mix was stunning. Its fur was soft—softer than the German Shepherds she was used to working with.

Pam examined the beast like she would any of her partners. Whoever owned this animal took excellent care of it.

She passed a hand along its belly, laughing when he jerked back.

"Oops, not a girl. Sorry about that. Still, I'd be glad for you to stick around if you don't have any big plans for the night."

She rose and the wolf stepped beside her heels. Very well trained, and to be honest, just the kind of company she needed after the strange ending to her evening.

Pam curled up in the corner of the couch. The wolf laid its chin on her knee and stared at her with a completely lovelorn expression. She rubbed his head again. She loved how completely honest and simple an animal's affection was. You could trust them to act according to normal patterns.

She missed her partner, but it had been time to let him retire.

"You like comedy or action movies better, wolfie? Come on, hop up. Maybe you're not allowed on the couch usually, but tonight is a special deal." She patted the seat beside her, and suddenly there was a large furry rug draping itself over her legs. She scratched his neck, checking for a collar and a dog tag. "I don't understand why the heck people don't collar their pets. What am I going to call you?"

A long wet tongue smeared its way up the side of her cheek, and she laughed out loud.

"Cool it, I don't need a bath." She grabbed him by the scruff of the neck and maneuvered him into a less accessible position. It might be a way of showing affection, but canine slobber wasn't her favourite.

She clicked the TV back on and tried to get into the show.

It was impossible. The edginess that had started earlier in the day still rode her hard. Damn TJ for getting her motor running then abandoning her. She tangled her fingers in the wolf's fur and tried to relax. The lingering heat of the day and the rest of the day's excitement finally got to her. Plus the warmth radiating from the wolf as he lay nestled alongside her.

There was something comforting about having an animal around. She missed her partner.

When she caught herself yawning for the third time in rapid succession she gave up, clicked off the screen and stretched lazily.

"Okay, wolfie. Time for you to head home." She rose to push open the kitchen door only to see the animal's rump disappear up the stairs. "Hey, where do you think you're going?"

When she found him curled up on her bed, she laughed. "Bet you're a bed hog. Fine, as long as you don't snore, you can stay."

She stripped off the sweats she'd changed into after abandoning the party before pulling on an oversized T-shirt. One hard shove moved him over enough she could crawl under the quilt.

He didn't do any of the usual canine things to settle down, just stuck his nose by her ear and licked her once before plopping on his belly close to her side. She chuckled and draped an arm over him.

Sometime during the night when she rolled over, he was gone.

How poetic, she'd been dumped by another male. She sighed and slipped back into her dreams.

4

———

Glorious blue sky greeted them for the first day of the tour. With the weather cooperating, Pam checked out the other hikers with a wary eye. This was the biggest concern she'd had with Maggie's suggestion she take part in an organized expedition—you never knew who your companions would be, and at times too many people made for trouble.

Keil called for everyone's attention before pointing at the stack of supplies piled on the picnic table.

"We've got light daypacks for everyone, already loaded with snacks and water bottles. Don't try to race up the hill. Take your time and enjoy the journey. There are a number of set places we'll stop and have photo ops, but anytime you need to stop and take a stretch break, feel free. We've got enough guides you can all go at your own pace."

Pam nodded in satisfaction. It appeared there were a few different fitness levels within the group, and while she wasn't sure how fast she'd be hiking, it was nice to know Keil didn't expect them to stick in one mass pack.

She stared up at King's Throne peak towering over her and adjusted the light pack to sit a little easier. Clear sky, soft fragrant breeze—should be an awesome day ahead.

She turned and bumped into TJ.

"Hey there, ready for the hike?"

She pretended to be annoyed. "Are you planning on dogging my heels the entire week I'm with the excursion?"

He wrinkled his nose. "Umm, pretty much the plan, yeah. Or at least until you accept my apology. I didn't mean to desert you the other night."

Pam laughed softly. The guy was nothing if not persistent. "I know, you were called away momentarily and when you got back I was gone. It's okay, I forgive you. Really."

"So why are you acting like you'd enjoy seeing me...fall in the lake or something?"

Tempting thought. Only because she bet he'd look great dripping wet, his clothes clinging to him. Maybe she could convince him it would be better to let them air dry and he would hike in the nude.

Yeah, right, with nine other people around?

He gestured down the path, and she fell into step with him. "I was upset, but I'm done. It just wasn't how I expected to spend the evening."

She heard his quick intake of air. Yeah, his response was pretty much her response.

She'd given it a lot of thought over the past two days as she got ready for the trip—especially after finding out TJ was one of the guides. She could stay mad and pout, or turn it around and have some fun. Since this was her chance to get out and have a good time, she chose to give him a break. There was too much attraction between them to be upset for any length of time, and really, wasn't it a waste of energy? She'd be gone in a couple of weeks, and in the meantime he could show her some Northern Hospitality.

But making him squirm was still fun.

They walked easily along the wide section of trail. "Is this an old road?"

"Logging road. The trail narrows when we reach the Cottonwood Junction. Then it's single file until we reach the meadow."

They chatted about the Yukon Territory. TJ pointed out some of the more unusual plants at their feet. "The wildflowers are pretty much all gone by now, except the fireweed."

"It's pretty."

"It's a weed, but yes, a pretty one."

Hours passed, and she fell into a rhythm, gazing out over the scenery and enjoying the chance for a physical challenge. A couple of the hikers in the group had fallen a fair ways behind, and soon there were only two others in the group with her and TJ.

"How long are you spending in the Yukon?" one of the men asked.

She slid a little farther away from him. While he wouldn't be a physical challenge to her, she didn't feel like flirting with anyone. Anyone other than TJ, that is.

"Couple of weeks, right?" TJ stepped between them before gesturing to the right and directing their attention to a lookout point.

Pam hid her smile.

The panoramic views when they reached the top were staggeringly beautiful. She wandered aimlessly and clicked picture after picture. Tufts of clouds clinging to the mountaintops. A ribbon of glacier ice trailing off into the distance. The sun reflecting in a million dazzling light spots on the surface of Kathleen Lake.

Every time she glanced up she found TJ's gaze fixed on her.

"Don't you have anyone else you need to take care of?"

He shook his head slowly. "I set up the picnic already, and everyone else is eating. I had to make sure you didn't stroll too close to the edge of the mountain or anything."

Oh dear, it was hot up here, under the blazing heat of his stare. "If there's a picnic, I guess I should go join them."

"I kept some out for us. We can eat here. Alone."

Pam concentrated hard. *Okey dokey.*

They sat together, TJ pointing in various directions and naming the local mountaintops visible from their vantage point. Pam nibbled on her sandwich, all the while trying to think of a good excuse to bring up the aborted kiss from the other night. As in, maybe they should find a way and means to try it again.

She'd never been so attracted to a man *and* so tongue-tied. There didn't seem to be any appropriate openings, and she wasn't about to simply jump him.

Well, not yet.

"So, I was thinking." TJ passed her a juice box, condensation beading its surface.

"Dangerous thing to do."

He grinned. "I'd like to make it up to you, I mean, leaving you in the lurch the other day. I kinda hoped you would forgive me enough to accept a little peace offering."

Hmmm, bribery totally worked. "Like extra chocolate bars? Dark? I'd be willing to forgive just about anything for chocolate."

His laugh rolled over her as he grabbed his daypack.

"That's not the surprise, but I think I can still help you out." He dug out a Ziploc bag and reached in for an extra-large foil-wrapped bar. "Oops, it's too warm today to be hauling chocolate. Sorry."

He pulled one out. Chocolate oozed from the edges and ran down his fingers. *Hello opportunity*. She grabbed his hand.

"No problem, I like it this way."

She brought his hand to her mouth and sucked one digit in, licking the warm, melted gooeyness clean before moving to the next one. His breathing sped up and her pussy grew wet.

Okay, she was over being mad, and there had better be private rooms available wherever they were staying tonight.

By the time she removed all traces of chocolate, she could barely breathe.

He leaned toward her, his dark eyes fixing her in place as their lips touched.

Bells rang. *Cool*, they weren't even kissing and she heard bells.

TJ pulled away with a sigh and her hopes faded. It was a real bell and it was moving closer. "There's the signal to round everyone up and start the journey down the hill." He stared at her lips. "Remember where we were..."

Oh boy.

Pam gathered her wits as best she could and scrambled to her feet. He aimed her in the right direction, and she shook her head as she hit the trail. Okay, he was fine enough looking, but she must have some kind of altitude fever.

She watched him out of the corner of her eye until he caught her.

Focus on the trail. There will be plenty of time to flirt later if I don't trip and break my neck.

Half an hour later he caught up with her, tugging gently on her hand to get her attention. "You interested in a little aerial sightseeing? My treat."

"You serious? When?"

TJ grinned and pulled her against him, hiding her from the others as they disappeared around the corner. He leaned closer and whispered in her ear. "In about an hour. I've arranged for a chopper to pick us up back in the meadow where we stopped for our first snack break this morning."

His warm breath caressed her neck, and a shiver raced over her skin. Holy hell, the man made her horny without even trying.

"So is this like a private event, or are we taking any of the others along as well?" She tilted her head to indicate the guy who had hit on her earlier.

"Very private. There's room for you and me and the pilot. So, you have to do a couple things. Number one." He kissed her neck and slipped his hand into her hair to nestle her a little closer.

"Number one?" Lordy, was that her voice? That throaty, sexy, fuck-me-in-the-meadow voice?

"Hmm, you can't tell anyone we're going." He nibbled on her earlobe and she moaned. *Oh yeah.*

"I can do that. I'm real good at keeping secrets."

"I bet you are. The second thing..." He stroked a hand down her back until he cupped her butt, and she was ready to crawl up his body.

"Second...*thing*. Damn it, TJ, you keep touching me and I won't remember a word you've said."

"All you need to remember is when the chopper lands, crouch low and come to the door quickly. We want to get away without upsetting the other customers too much, okay?"

"Are you going to get in trouble for this?"

He didn't answer, just tugged her closer and took her lips.

Lordy, the guy could kiss. His lips alone started reactions that other lovers had to work up to with a full dinner, dance and a couple of bottles of wine. When he finally broke off, she had to gasp for air.

He smiled at her, his thumb brushing her cheek gently. "Some troubles are completely worth the risk."

He drew apart and held a finger to his lips. She nodded. It would be nice to be able to get away from the group. She'd flown in choppers, but only for work. Excitement made her shiver.

"Where are we going to go?"

"Fly over a bit of the Kluane National Park. You'll be able to see Mount Logan before we'll head over the glacier field and past a couple of beautiful lakes."

She grabbed his hand and squeezed it. "Thanks, TJ. This is very considerate. I'm looking forward to spending a little time alone with you." His eyes flashed dark and he gazed the length of her body before dragging himself away.

"Remember that. Time alone is a good thing."

TJ LISTENED INTENTLY for the sound of the chopper. It was going to all come down to timing. The pilot was a friend of his, and hopefully Shaun had managed to get everything in place.

Now to make sure Keil didn't interrupt his plans.

The group had spread out like they usually did by this time during a hike. The more eager people had stayed high to do a little extra exploring. Keil had begun the downward journey with the slower-moving crew to give them extra time to make it to the parking lot and the picnic supper being prepared for them.

Pam took a swallow from her water bottle and licked her lips, and his cock jerked to life again. He'd been pretty much hard since two nights ago when she'd stripped in front of him. The memory of her naked torso before she'd pulled on a sleep shirt—the image was as clear as a picture and it haunted him. His mate was exactly what he desired in a woman. He'd had to leave before he was too tempted to shift out of his wolf and crawl all over her.

No, this was far better. Time alone. That was the goal, wasn't it? He heard the faint sound of Shaun's chopper in the distance grow nearer.

"Come on, let's head to the edge of the meadow."

She took his hand, and he had to ignore the electric shock that flew through him. He wondered if his touch had the same effect on her as on him. There was no doubt in his mind they would be fabulous together. Not just sex, although, hello, that was looking to be spectacular as well, but she seemed so understanding and he was looking forward to the next week. Finding out what it meant to have someone to lavish all his attention on. All his love.

He needed to pull off one last maneuver.

The volume and wind movement increased as the helicopter hovered overhead, and Pam hid her face against his chest. His arm around her shoulders felt so good and natural he knew there must be a big goofy grin on his face.

He protected her until the runners settled and the door swung open.

His friend Jared jumped out, flashed a thumbs-up and sprinted to the edge of the field. TJ guided Pam and popped her into the cabin, climbed after her and shut the door firmly. She searched for seatbelts and he reached to help her, then tapped Shaun on the shoulder. When the clamor of the props increased to painful decibels, he grabbed the headsets hanging on the sidewall. After slipping hers on, he showed her the buttons to press to talk.

"You comfy?" He rearranged the daypacks at their feet, leaning closer under the disguise of adjusting her seatbelt.

"Great. Where are we headed?"

Paradise, he hoped. "Look out the left window, there's Mount Logan. Almost twenty thousand feet or six thousand metres, it's the tallest in Canada and second tallest in North America."

She leaned across his body to see out his side window and her hair fell like a curtain across him. Sweet smelling. A combination of jasmine and her own natural scent. The one that made his eyes cross and his pants grow far too tight.

"Gorgeous. Is that the glacier you mentioned?"

He pointed out the other window, wrapped his arm around her and carried on with the tour. Every trip he'd done over the past years came in handy as he managed to answer most of her questions.

The tour also helped time to pass. Once out of Kluane National Park, they dipped around Sheep Mountain, leaving behind the Alaskan highway to head deeper into the bush. Thick forest spread under them, rising and falling in endless green waves. Shaun gestured in the air and TJ's excitement rose. They were almost there. He squeezed Pam's fingers. Somehow her hand had found its way into his and he didn't want to let go.

"You want to land?" he asked her.

She grinned at him. "You mean it?"

Outside the window was the foot of a pristine mountain lake, a field of wild grasses stretching from the shore toward the tree-covered foothills of the mountain. Shaun maneuvered his way to the north where a sparkling brook raced into the lake. He settled the chopper in a small meadow, and TJ cracked open the door, hopped out and reached to help Pam.

Of course, when she lost her balance and landed on top of him he was torn between cursing his bad luck and longing to stay there forever.

Stick to the plan. "It's noisy here. Let's move a bit."

"Is he going to stop the propellers?"

Highly unlikely, but he wasn't going to tell her that. Yet. She laughed as he rolled, bringing her to her feet and running away from the chopper until they could speak without shouting.

"Do we have long enough I can go touch the lake?"

"Sure." He followed her, and she spun her arms out in a circle, breathing in huge drafts of the air. She looked wild and alive and vital, and he was head-over-heels in love.

"Race you." She was off.

TJ chased her, catching her before they lost the grass underfoot. He tackled her carefully, twisting as they fell to put her in his arms, resting on top of him.

It took a second for the utter shock of having succeeded without breaking bones, his or hers, to fully register.

"Well, hello. Weren't we here a couple of minutes ago?" Pam teased, resting her elbows on his chest and cradling her chin in her hands.

"I think we were *almost* here. There's one thing missing."

He cupped her head and lowered her lips to his. Her taste twined around him and sucked him under, the feel of his mate resting on top of him the best thing he'd ever experienced.

She responded with enthusiasm, exploring with her tongue, kissing him back with as much passion as he wished. She pulled her legs up to straddle him and her warm crotch rested on his groin. A faint movement of her hips and the contact increased.

Oh hell, he was going to explode if she wiggled again.

Pam sat upright, the highlights in her hair shining red in the sun's bright light. She grinned at him. "Well, I seem to have you at my mercy, but we probably need to be going soon, right?"

The loudening *flap flap* of the propeller blades reached them, and her eyes widened. "What's he doing?"

She scrambled to the side, and her jaw fell open as the chopper lifted. The air pressure flattened them to the ground as Shaun got away.

TJ waved at his friend as the aircraft rose, hovering over the field for a moment before rotating and taking off into the distance.

"What is going on? Stop it...come back." Pam ran after the helicopter, waving her arms frantically before returning, her beautiful brown eyes wide. "He left us. What is he doing?"

TJ stood and pulled her back into his arms. "Don't worry, it's okay. He'll be back."

She relaxed. "Well, that's good. How long do we have before he returns?"

"A week."

5

***P**am stared at him. What kind of...? It had to be a joke.

"No, seriously. Does he need to get fuel or something?"

"Nope, he's got a few other things to do, but he'll be back for us. Eventually. You want to help me carry our packs to the cabin?" TJ turned to step toward the center of the meadow.

Cabin? She grabbed him by the arm and whipped him to face her. "You're shitting me, aren't you? You really just had us dumped in the bush? Are you *insane?*"

"Look, it's going to be fine. Let's grab our stuff and we can talk about it more once we're settled."

She bit her tongue. Seriously, the guy must not have been firing on all rockets, but humouring him for a moment was the only solution. She stared around the meadow a little more intently. "Where is everything? The cabin, the food, the bathhouse with the running water and satellite TV?"

"No TV, but I do promise running water. Come on."

He led her to the spot the helicopter had landed. There, where the grass lay low from the air from the propellers compressing it flat, sat a box and two full-sized backpacks. One of them was her own bright red pack she could have sworn she'd left safely back at the expedition van.

He shouldered his pack and the box, grinned at her and led her toward the trees.

Okay. She was going to kill him, but after she had a roof over her head. She shrugged on her pack and followed behind.

The trail led to a neat log cabin facing the lake. It was tucked in so tight she hadn't even noticed it earlier, but now she appreciated the setting. Once she got past the part of her that wanted to take TJ apart, this wasn't a bad place.

He stopped at the bottom of the wide staircase leading up to the sturdy wood door.

"A private getaway just for you. I know I should have checked with you first, but I needed to make things happen pretty quick. I figured asking for forgiveness would be easier than asking permission."

She stared at him in disbelief. This wasn't happening. Her heart pounded, blood rushing past her temples so hard her vision blurred. She wasn't sure if it was from shock or because she was pissed off.

Pissed off. Definitely the one to go with. The man needed to be handled, and she had the touch. Pam calmed her expression and spoke softly.

"So what you're trying to tell me is you deliberately set this up. The remote cabin, the whole 'just us by ourselves' thing?"

He nodded, a twinkle in his eye.

"Ahhh, that's so..." She stepped closer and patted him on the cheek. "How incredibly..."

With one quick movement she grabbed his ear and twisted, hard.

He clutched her hand and dropped to his knees. "Shit, wait."

She glared daggers at him. "I can't believe you're such a *schmuck*. Who in the hell put you in charge of me? Did you ask? Did you even consider maybe what I signed up for was what I wanted to take part in? Idiot."

An extra twist accompanied her final word and TJ yowled through clenched teeth.

"Arghhh, I have the list of all the things you wanted to try. We'll make it happen here, only a little more enjoyable because there won't be crowds around."

She let go of his ear and stomped across the porch. Unbelievable. "You *kidnapped* me."

"Wait, it's not like that." He scrambled to his feet, patting all his pockets frantically. "Ah, fuck, I'm screwing this all up. I didn't say it right. I meant to... I wanted to *ask* you if you would like to stay here. We can still call the helicopter back. Just..."

TJ tossed the pack off his back and flipped open zippers, obviously looking for something. Pam lowered her pack as well, dropping it against the side of the cabin. She wanted her hands and feet clear if she needed to kick his butt. She assumed a defensive crouch, ready to smack him to the ground if necessary.

He twirled toward her. Something dark thrust her direction and she moved instinctively, the side of her hand cracking his forearm hard enough to bruise. As he cried out, an oblong shape flew from his fingers and slammed into the door. Pieces of black plastic rained down on the porch boards, a set of batteries rolling and spinning back from the wall, finally coming to a stop against her foot.

Fuck.

Pam knelt and picked up the mangled body of the transceiver, snapped wires dangling from the case. One round dial fell to the ground and spun like a top, the echo of the *whirl whirl* fading until the piece tipped over with a soft *plop*.

TJ cleared his throat.

She pinned her lips together. Letting out a shriek of laughter right now probably wasn't the most mature response, but...oh my God. It was a full minute before she could speak.

"That was a satellite phone?" She was proud of how calm she sounded. Not on the verge of hysteria or anything.

"Umm, right. So we could call Shaun back if you didn't want to stay."

Pam closed her eyes and counted to ten. Two wrongs didn't make a right, but it appeared his mistake coupled with hers did make them stranded.

"That was our only phone?"

"Yup."

His honest answer amused the heck out of her and suddenly most of her bluster drained away. "I'm upset with you. Don't get me wrong, I'm still planning on getting my revenge. But in a kind of twisted way, you bringing me here is sweet. Psycho, but sweet."

"Twisted and sweet. I'll take it." He gave her the most disarming puppy-dog look, and she bit her lip to stop from laughing.

He opened the door and motioned for her to enter first.

She grabbed her pack, crunching a couple of pieces of plastic underfoot as she stepped inside. The cabin was bright and cheery, and bigger than she'd expected. The main area held an open sitting room with a mini kitchen on one side and a beautiful stone fireplace on the opposite wall.

Two doors opened off the back, and after dropping her pack to the floor, she peeked her head into the first to find a bedroom. Damn, that wasn't a king-size either, more like a king plus.

"I have to do a couple of things outside. Look around, get settled." TJ took off quickly and she let out a big breath.

Holy crap, they were stuck here. She should be absolutely furious. How could anyone in this day and age think it was okay to take a person somewhere without permission?

Yet as she wandered the cabin, she wasn't really upset. She had wanted to have an adventure, and signing up for the expedition had been more Maggie's idea than her own.

It was partly her fault for overreacting on the stairs. Oh God. She laughed at herself, shaking her head as she wandered the cabin. This—enforced solitude—was what she truly wanted right now. Add the fact that TJ, Mr. Turns-me-on-without-even-trying, was the one she was staying with?

She stared at the monstrous bed again. Okay. She was the one out of her mind, but this could actually be a lot of fun.

Of course she still planned on making him suffer. She should be able to get a few backrubs, maybe even a foot massage, out of him if he felt guilty enough.

She spotted a broom in the corner and took a few passes, but there wasn't anything underfoot that shouldn't be there. She checked the cupboards, looked under the bed...no dust, no signs of mice. The cupboards were full with dry goods and snacks. It was the cleanest cabin she'd ever seen. Cleaner than her apartment since Maggie moved out, if she was honest.

Heavy footsteps landed on the porch boards, and she hurried out of the bedroom to see TJ shoulder his way into the front room, his arms around a paper bag. He watched her closely and she sighed.

"I'm not going to hit you over the head with the cast-iron frying pan I found, if that's what you're worried about."

He grinned. "Good, because we'll need that for breakfast, and pancakes cook better in undented pans."

She laughed. "Okay, we'll talk about the abduction in more detail later. Can I help you put things away?"

The bottom of the paper bag he held gave way, sending the contents to the floor in a cascading avalanche. They both scrambled to catch things, but in the end most of it ended up in a heap at their feet. She bent to help gather the scented candles, chocolates, massage oil, extra-large box of condoms...

Heat raced over her as she held it up, staring at his bright red face. "Got plans?"

He swallowed a few times nervously. "Only if you do."

Oh lordy. She needed to regain a little control, and holding the evidence of what could happen very shortly was not making this any easier. She stepped back. "I think... I need some fresh air."

"Why don't you let me clean up and put stuff away? You can go..."

"I'll check out the lake..."

They spoke simultaneously. It was too much, and she fled, racing out the door to where the evening breeze carried over the water.

Two more seconds and she would have had him using one of the condoms.

The trail straight in front of the cabin led her to a tiny dock extending over the water. She pulled off her shoes and dangled her feet in the cool liquid.

She worked hard and played hard, and this being out of control was not what she liked in her life. She'd sworn long ago that *she* would be the one to call the shots. Yet here she was, totally out of her comfort zone, and the sensation creeping up her spine wasn't fear, or dismay, but delight.

Why?

Pam reclined back on the dock and closed her eyes. The sunlight hit her face, its fading heat still enough to help her relax. She was trapped here for the week. There was no way she would be stupid enough to try to get out of the bush alone, so she had two choices. Whine about it, or hop in with both feet. Have a great time with the guy, then take the memories with her when she left.

She needed a break right now anyway. With her partner retired, she had to train a new one, and she had a month's leave coming. Time to set some new goals for her life. Twenty-six, and already feeling like she might be alone forever.

But not this week. Whether he realized it or not, TJ had hit her right when she needed this most. She sat up and kicked the water, splashing and raising a ruckus. Life should be enjoyed, and she had every intention of enjoying it to the hilt for this week.

The sun slipped behind the mountaintop, casting a shadow across the lake and she breathed in the clear air. It was definitely a place to make some memories.

TJ WATCHED HER, his wolf poking him to go to her side. She seemed so small and alone sitting on the dock, and he was a little worried he'd pushed it too hard bringing her here. Hopefully the next days would be enough for him to convince her he was a forever kind of guy.

When she threw back her head and laughed, splashing like a child, he had to fight back the urge to run and join her.

All his life he'd longed to have the kind of connection he'd seen in others of the pack. How it would work with him being a wolf and her human, he still didn't know, but there was no one else who had ever made him feel this way.

Groveling about to commence.

He approached slowly, but she heard him. Turning her body, she pulled her legs up and wrapped her arms around her knees. She smiled at him and the warmth hit him like a two-by-four between the eyes.

"You getting hungry?" he asked.

She nodded. "By the way, are you going to tell me where we are?"

"Northwest of Haines Junction, on one of the northern arms of Kluane Lake. The cabin is a friend's, and he and his wife have gone south visiting family."

"How did you get everything here? It's clean and stocked and everything."

"Shaun, the helicopter pilot. He came in earlier, brought supplies and cleaned up for us."

The streak of mischief lighting her face was slightly frightening. "You seem to have brought a few supplies of your own."

He coughed. "About that... I didn't mean to presume, and it's totally up to you if we..."

Pam rose to her feet and stretched, and his mouth watered. Her breasts pressed against the front of her T-shirt, the muscles of her arms reflecting the glowing light of the setting sun. She stepped nearer.

"Don't presume, but I do like you. I'm pretty interested myself, as I think you could tell from the other night. So don't get all shy and shit on me. Do you want me?"

Oh my God. "More than you could possibly know."

She licked her lips as she checked him over. "Looks like we might have an interesting week ahead of us. Only your list of activities? I want to see what you've got planned. I wanted a northern experience, and you're going to give it to me, right?"

Oh yeah, he'd give her anything she wanted.

He held out his hand. "Supper first? Then we'll plan tomorrow?"

She took his fingers into hers and clasped them tightly.

Dishes were done, the fireplace crackled, and TJ couldn't keep his eyes off her.

"Thanks for supper."

He snorted. "I should have warned you, I'm not that good a cook."

"Hey, mac and cheese with all the ketchup I wanted? What more is needed?" She held out her wine glass and he topped it up. "Your buddy Shaun did a fine job with the supplies."

He stared at her a little longer. The smooth sweep of her cheek, the way her hair hung over her skin and shone with the light. She was gorgeous and he ached for her.

"You want to play a game?" He needed something to distract him from stripping her and burying himself in her body before she was ready. Her scent filled the room, and he had to concentrate hard to stop from drooling.

"A game? Sure." She put down her wine glass and crawled into his lap, and he nearly swallowed his tongue.

"What...what are you doing?" *Holy shit.* She unbuttoned the top of his shirt and leaned in to press a kiss to his neck.

"Trying to decide what game to play."

It was hard to hear with the blood rushing past his ears en route from leaving his brain to congregate in more southerly regions. When she sat up and stripped off her T-shirt, he squeezed his eyes shut tight, locking his fingers through the belt loops on her shorts. He was not going to rush her. She could set the pace.

"Hmm, I'd say strip poker, but I'm really bad at cards, so that wouldn't last very long." He didn't dare peek, but her hands were back on him. She finished the rest of his buttons and slipped the shirt from his shoulders.

He leaned forward to let her maneuver the garment the rest of the way off, and his chest hit her breasts. Her naked, hot, bare breasts.

His eyes popped open. "Oh, sweet mercy, you're killing me."

"Why would you say that?" She cupped herself, rolling her nipples between thumb and forefinger, and stars floated in front of his vision.

"Pam, are you sure? We don't have to do this, not tonight."

That wasn't him talking. Some stranger had abducted him. *He* would have been touching her, smoothing her skin, reaching out to lap at the pale pink circles peaking her breasts. He wouldn't be stupid enough to try to slow her down, or heaven forbid, stop her from shifting slightly upward and bringing her nipple in contact with his lips.

Just a taste. He licked lightly, and the tip hardened under his tongue. Her flavour rolled through him, intoxicating and rich. He closed his lips and sucked.

"Yes. Oh, *yes.*" Pam dragged her fingers through his hair and held him close, and there was no stopping the train. He switched from side to side, feasting on her body, the crackle of the fire fading as her cries increased in volume. She was loud and vocal, and while he'd never had trouble making the ladies happy in bed, knowing what turned his mate on was the most awe-inspiring feeling he'd ever experienced.

He cupped her butt and stood, shuffling toward the bedroom as she latched onto his lips. Walking blind, he bumped into the doorframe a couple of times until he made it through and backed to the edge of the bed. He lowered her to the firm surface and stepped back to stare.

Her dark hair spread over the light-coloured comforter, her lips wet from their kisses, her bare torso enticing. She unsnapped her waist button and opened the zipper, and he couldn't breathe. Could barely think as she wiggled out of her shorts and undies.

Naked.

Waiting.

His wolf howled with delight. His mate wanted him. Was waiting for him. He stepped closer and fell to his knees. One firm pull brought her hips to the end of the mattress. He opened her legs and kissed her intimately.

She laughed, and it turned into a moan as he extended his tongue and licked her slit, separating her curls and finding her wet and ready.

His cock ached behind his clothing, but he was glad for the distraction. He wanted to make this special for her. Their first time, first of forever as far as he was concerned. He tasted her again, reveling in her gasps, the breathy moans escaping her throat as he circled her clit with his tongue.

When he slid a finger into her sheath and suckled at the same time, she cried out and came, her body responding far too quickly. It wasn't enough, not nearly enough pleasure.

He refused to stop, holding her down when she wiggled. One hand stilled her hips as he continued to lick and suck, pumping two fingers into her core, massaging her sheath.

"You're killing me. Too sensitive, it's too much."

He lifted his head to soak in the sight. Her cheeks were flushed, her eyes glazed. She took a deep, shaky breath and his heart expanded. That response was because of *him*. Because of what he was doing to her.

"Never enough. I want you to come again before I sink into you. Before it's not my fingers filling you up, but my cock joining us together."

She screwed her eyes shut and hissed. Her pussy was wet and the intimate sounds of his fingers thrusting filled the air. When she came this time, it was with a contented sigh, and he dropped his head on her belly and shivered with how intensely satisfied it made him feel to please his mate.

He slowed his fingers, caressing the entrance to her body softly. Circling the delicate tissues as she continued to convulse under him. He rose and joined her, kissing her tenderly, rolling her to the side as she buried her hands in his hair.

Long breathless moments later she pulled back, stroking his cheek, her gaze darting over his face.

"Thank you, that was amazing."

"We're not done." He lowered his head and took her lips again. He couldn't get enough of her mouth, the scent and taste of her filling his head and making him crazy. She tugged on his pants, pushing the fabric over his hips, her soft hands caressing the bare skin of his butt. His cock touched her warm leg, and he shuddered, fighting for control.

"Lift up," she whispered, and then, sweet mercy, she had her hands on his cock and he was going to die. He nestled his face against her throat, soaking in every sensation—the scent of her skin, the aching pleasure in his balls as she somehow, from somewhere, rolled a condom onto his shaft.

He wished the damn thing were a million miles away. He wanted to take his mate, skin on skin. Needed to feel her wetness around him. Her warmth enclosing him, but he'd known that wouldn't work. So the condom it was, and even as he ached for what he couldn't have, she shifted under him, opening her legs, and the head of his cock breached her pussy.

"Take me." Pam arched against him and he slid in a bit farther.

With pleasure. He slipped in slowly, savouring the sensation of her clasp around him until he was buried to the hilt. She was tight and wet and holy-fucking-moly nothing had ever felt like this before.

He stared into her big brown eyes. Anchored on his elbows, one on either side of her, their bodies joined together, a slow and seductive dance of pleasure. The hint of a smile appeared at the corner of her mouth, and he kissed it. Kissed his way across her cheek and back to her neck. He wanted to bite her so badly his gums ached.

Wanted to mark her as his and make sure no matter what happened he would have that connection with her, but he couldn't. Not until she knew *everything*.

Somewhere he found the strength to simply lick her jugular, ignoring the pounding pulse under his mouth. He concentrated on dragging his cock in and out of her sweet body.

Pam wrapped her legs around him, and on the next pass, he sank a little deeper and she made a little sound that made his balls tighten.

"So good. Oh yeah, right there." She swore a couple of times, and he laughed.

"What's good, this?" He slid over her clit. It must have been sensitive from his earlier ministrations, and her eyes rolled back a little. "Yup, that's what I thought."

"Faster," she demanded, tugging with her feet against his ass.

He chuckled and dropped to suck on her nipples, nipping lightly with his teeth, soothing the rigid peaks with his tongue. "Slower."

He was going numb from the waist down, which, when added to how confused and crazy she made his mind, turned the whole situation a little cloudy and surreal. He didn't want it to end, didn't want to speed up, but the tingling ache at the base of his spine warned he wasn't going to last forever. He kissed her again, taking her mouth and commanding her attention. He plunged as deep as possible, pressing her against the bed so hard it squeaked, her breath rushing past his cheek as he reached down and slipped a hand between them.

"Come for me again. One more time. Squeeze me in that sweet pussy of yours until I can't stand it anymore."

He pressed on her clit in time with his thrusts. Pam clutched his neck in a death grip, and when she moaned out in pleasure, he closed his eyes and slammed in. Again and again as her body clutched him, waves convulsing around him. He hung on to his control by a thread. Then her hot mouth and seeking lips closed on his neck, and she bit him.

He exploded into her depths.

6

*S*orry guys, I didn't get anything useful out of Jared. TJ was very smart—all he told Jared was he planned on taking his vacation a little early and didn't want to leave the excursion in the lurch, could Jared fill in for a few days? He knows nothing more.

Find Shaun. He's the one who took them away. Check Granite Lake cabin, check the usual hangouts. I'm trapped taking care of this booking. When I find that boy I'm going to skin him alive. Robyn, you said you wanted a new rug for the living room, right?

Keil

BLISS.

Why had she never done this before? The totally decadent adoration of a slightly younger guy was awesome. Here she'd been going out with older men thinking that being more mature they would know their way around a girl's pink parts better, but TJ?

Whoa Nelly, the guy had talented fingers.

Even now he was using them to her best advantage. Last night had rocked, and she couldn't quite remember when she'd fallen asleep. Somewhere between their third and fourth tumble on the bed, things got blurry, but the drag of his hands down her back as he massaged her naked body this morning was very clear.

Bliss.

Or had she thought that already?

He pressed harder, his thumbs sinking into the tight muscles in her lower back and she groaned. "Oh yeah, right there."

"Hmm, sleeping beauty awakes. I seem to remember you saying that a lot last night."

"Oh yeah?"

"And the 'right there'. You're very vocal in bed. I like that." He kissed her cheek and lay next to her, the warmth of his bare skin covering her in lieu of the quilt.

"Don't see any good reason to be shy."

He watched her with the strangest expression on his face.

She leaned up on one elbow. "What?"

"How do you feel?"

"Well fucked."

He frowned and stared in silence for a minute.

"Am I supposed to feel something else? You're a seriously good lover, TJ. I'm happy as a clam, or I would be if you'd get back to what you were doing a minute ago." She caught a flash of sadness in his eyes, but as curious as it made her, deep introspection before she'd brushed her teeth was not in the books. "Hey, did you tell me there's a shower?"

He kissed her nose before sitting up and resuming his magic touch on her body.

"Massage first. You can shower while I'm cooking breakfast. The water heater is a rapid-fire system, and I turned on the pump last night. With a lake full of water and the propane generator, you can have as long a shower as you want."

"This place is not nearly as rustic as it appears at first glance."

"Only the best for you."

She laughed. "So glad you had my comfort in mind when you shanghaied me." She lay back to enjoy what the day would hold.

THEY SAT OVERLOOKING the lake while a delicious sensation of fatigue stole through her limbs. Private excursions by *Kidnappers R Us* for the win. "Other than warning you I'm taking over the cooking, this day has been incredible. I loved the canoeing, and the hike to the lookout was fabulous."

"Sorry about the grilled cheese sandwiches at lunch."

"Hey, a little carbon is supposed to be good for the system, right? Clears it out."

TJ smiled at her as he touched her hair. He'd been doing that all day long. Stroking her cheek, holding her hand. Even with him acting like some kind of weird stalker, she couldn't muster any concern. It was all so innocent, and tender.

"I'm very thankful you've been so understanding about me...well..."

"The kidnapping? Forget it. I tried to get upset, but somewhere at about the fifteenth orgasm all my ability to be freaked out seemed to float away."

"You haven't come that many times."

She laughed softly. "Well, then, you'd better get busy, hadn't you?"

He moved closer, wrapped an arm behind her and let her lean against him. "Tonight. Right now, enjoy the view. I know I am."

"You're not even looking around." Pam flushed. The man never seemed to take his eyes off her. "You're staring again."

"I know."

"It's very flattering."

TJ tugged her head against his chest and she relaxed, letting him support her weight as they watched the sun approach the top of the mountain. Under her ear his heart pulsed evenly, the solid beat lulling her into a lazy state.

"You think you'd like to live up north?" he asked.

She'd thought about it, but moving wasn't practical. "It's pretty, but my job is down south. I need to get ready to train a new partner."

"Partner?"

"RCMP, remember? My partner retired, and I'll need to go start the process again." She sighed. "Damon was awesome. I miss him a lot."

A strange choking cough shook TJ. "Damon?"

"Yeah. We were inseparable. Even the coldest nights were fine because he would warm me up." TJ tensed under her, and Pam turned toward him. His face was bright red and his lips were moving, but no sound was coming out. "You okay?"

He shook his head and cleared his throat a few times. "I'll be fine. I've never had a woman tell me about an old lover like this, while we're—"

"Lover?" *What the hell? Oh shit.* A laugh burst out. By the time she'd regained control, her stomach was sore and she was gasping for air.

It didn't help that every time she looked at TJ his expression set her off again.

"Sorry...don't mean to be rude. Oh my God, you're kidding me. Didn't you know? Damon was my partner, but he's a *dog*."

"That's my opinion for sure."

"No, seriously, a German Shepherd. I'm a dog handler for the Royal Canadian Mounted Police. Narcotics division, and I double in Search and Rescue when needed."

"You're a dog handler?" He collapsed back onto the blanket, his arms flung out to the side. "Oh man, I am never going to live this one down."

Pam crawled nearer, resting her head on his chest. There was something very comfortable about the position. "I know, it's a bit of a surprise, but I'm not sure why you think it's such an odd job. It's been a great way to be involved in the RCMP and still be able to enjoy working with animals. I debated training as a vet, but with one thing and another, it didn't work out."

TJ rolled her, leaning close to nuzzle her neck, and the rising anticipation she was coming to expect around him seized her again. He spoke quietly, the brush of air from his lips teasing her ear. "I think it's a fabulous job, and I bet you are completely awesome. All the dogs must have contests to figure out who gets you as their partner."

"Goof."

"Just saying…"

She chuckled then broke into a huge yawn. What an amazing day. TJ tangled his fingers in her hair to stroke and pet her, and she wrapped her arms around his neck to encourage him closer.

He took the hint and kissed her. Slow and thorough. Damn, he tasted good. It was like he knew exactly what kind of mood she was in. Tired from their busy day, she felt dreamy and soft, and that's how he kissed her.

He pulled back and his eyes sparkled, the dark centers mesmerizing. "As pleasurable as this is, I need to make sure I tied the canoe properly. I have a sneaky suspicion I forgot, and I don't want to have to go for a swim tomorrow to find it."

"You want me to come with you?"

"You can, or you can stay here. I'll only be a minute."

She waved him off as another yawn escaped. She lay back on the blanket. Oh yeah, she was totally into this holiday. Six more days? They should think about getting an extension.

She covered her eyes with her arm and breathed in deeply. The clean air filled her lungs with a fresh energy. She wondered what new tricks they could get up to tonight. Maybe make love in front of the fire.

Something inside paused. Since when did she call it making love? Sex was sex. You took care of your partner, had some fun then moved on.

A rustling in the nearby trees made her sit up, and she watched carefully for signs of what made the noise. They hadn't spotted any wildlife yet, and that was one thing she hoped to change before heading home.

She stood to have a better view. The lower limbs of a bush wiggled. Something small. The sound of sniffing reached her ears and she hesitated.

That didn't sound like a deer or a caribou or some other four-legged vegetarian. The head that popped out from the forest was brown washed with streaks of grey. One plate-sized paw followed another and Pam froze in terror.

Bear.

Oh my God, what was she supposed to do? She racked her brain for the training session she'd taken on bear encounters, but it had been a long time ago. *Stay still. It can't see me if I don't move.*

No, wait—that's what you're supposed to do for a T-Rex.

There was still a fair distance between her and the bear, so she took a cautious step backward. The animal's head pivoted in her direction and it sniffed harder.

Pam clenched her teeth together to stop them from chattering.

The animal reared on its hind legs, scenting the air. It snorted at her, twice.

She took another step backward and spoke softly. "Go away. I'm human. I'm not interesting at all. Oh damn, *damn, damn,* TJ, this is a rotten time to be out strolling." Sneaking a peek over her shoulder to see if there was any action by the lake tempted her, but that would have required taking her eyes off the bear and *that* was physically impossible.

The beast wavered, its upper body rocking from side to side for a second before it suddenly dropped to all fours, and with a nerve-racking grumble, it rushed her. She shouted, adrenaline flashing through her veins.

She looked around frantically for a stick or a rock or anything to defend herself, but there was nothing at hand, and besides, her limbs were frozen in terror.

A blur of silver fur flew past her from behind. She stumbled back and swore as she identified a canine-like body darting at the bear. Her attacker jerked to a stop, and snarled, its teeth gnashing together before spinning around.

It disappeared into the bush with a crash, the wolf hard on its heels. A loud howl rang out as her protector paused at the tree line before pacing over to sit a short distance from her feet.

Pam wrapped her arms around herself to stop the shaking from taking over even as she stared at the animal.

How in the world?

"Wolfie?"

7

─────────

*K*eil,

Granite Lake is empty. There's no sign of him at any of the pack's summer retreats. We even checked the old-timer's trapline cabins and came up blank. As for Shaun, he did a supply run up north to Old Crow then parked the chopper and said he was taking a week-long vacation. The locals saw him head into the bush with a backpack. Looks like he's the only one who knows where Pam and TJ are, and he's making sure no Alpha can contact him and order him to spill the beans.

I discovered a couple of the other single guys in the pack put together a food package for TJ. Seems he called in favours from all his buddies. All they can say is TJ asked for help, and no one turns him down.

BTW, Maggie texted. She said you don't have to worry about Pam suing us, but you might not get a chance to skin TJ. Pam is very capable of handing out her own chastisement. Did you remember she's an RCMP? You're going to die when you hear the division she works in.

Robyn

~

Shit.

Shit.

Pam was totally going to kill him. And after that, Keil was going to rip off his fur and use him for trimming coats.

Halfway back from the lake he'd spotted the bear rearing before her. It was probably just trying to figure out what she was—bears had rotten eyesight—but he wasn't sure Pam knew it simply wanted to catch her scent.

And while there was no reason for it to really attack, he couldn't risk her misunderstanding if it made a false rush forward. His wolf demanded he take action, and before he knew it he had stripped, shifting as he ran to convince ol' Bruin to hightail it off for a different patch of berries.

TJ moved slowly toward Pam who stared around in confusion. She yelled his name a few times. "TJ! You *jerk,* get your butt up here."

She was a freaking dog handler. How was he supposed to talk to her?

For the millionth time he wished they were completely mated like full-blood wolves. That he could talk to her mind and have her hear his voice.

"Okay, you look like the pet wolf I met at Maggie's. But that's flipping impossible. Stay."

He froze. Anything to make her more comfortable.

"Shit, you're not supposed to be trained. How did you get here? Come." She snapped her fingers, and TJ trotted to her side as she continued to call his name loudly in the direction of the lake.

His internal debate continued. If he ran into the trees and doubled back behind the cabin, he could shift and pretend to have been in there the whole time. Except that would explain his absence, but not the presence of the "wolfie", and it would be a lie.

He didn't want to lie to her. Didn't want to keep up the deception. He ached to tell her everything, and following at her heels as she ran to the cabin, he made his decision. He was going to show her.

Maybe it was too soon. But...they'd hit it off, right? Surely it would be better to be honest now instead of coming clean later and having the lies held over his head. She pushed open the door and searched the cabin.

"TJ, where in the hell are you?"

He blocked her path when she would have left the cabin, nudging her instead toward the couch.

"Stop it, I need to find TJ."

He forced his body weight against her legs to make her move the direction he wanted, and suddenly sharp pain radiated out from his ear, followed by his throat, as she put him into a chokehold.

"Stay."

Okay, enough of her ordering him around like a dog. He hesitated for all of two seconds before shifting back into his human form.

～

PAM'S HEART rate hovered around three hundred beats per minute. It had shot up there when the bear appeared and pretty much stayed at that level all the way until the damn dog blocked her path.

Fuck this, she needed to get out of the building and no animal was going to stop her.

Of course, feeling the fur under her elbow change to human skin and discovering she clutched the ear of a naked TJ did things to her blood pressure she was pretty sure were dangerous.

She released him and slammed back into the door.

TJ rose to his feet and stepped away from her, his hands held out non-threateningly.

"What. The hell. Just. Happened," she shouted.

He cringed.

Okay, maybe she was a few decibels over the safety levels, but...*fuck.*

"I can explain," TJ insisted.

Pam gasped for air. She wasn't sure if she was going to throw up or laugh. Her stomach rolled a little more, and she would have closed her eyes, but she wanted to make sure she knew where he was at all times.

"Start now. Make it snappy."

TJ glanced down at his naked body. "Can I pull on some clothes?"

She nodded. Even while freaking out she found him distractingly attractive.

He turned and disappeared into the bedroom they'd shared last night, his naked butt teasing her.

He'd turned into a wolf. That wasn't possible.

TJ returned and dug into the cooler, poured a glass of something and gestured for her to sit on the couch. She had to peel herself off the door.

"You planning on..." She couldn't think what to accuse him of. He'd turned into a freaking *wolf*.

He held out the glass. "Orange juice. The calories are supposed to be good for people who have had a shock. Damn it, Pam, I'm really sorry. I didn't mean to spill the beans this way. The bear wasn't going to hurt you. I mean, I know that must have been freaky to have him run at you like that, but that's called a bluff, because this time of year he'd be more interested in the berries. He just wanted to scare you off, but I still needed to make sure you were safe, and I know it's a lot to take in—" He slammed his lips together and motioned with the glass. "Please, you'll feel better."

She sat across from him and sipped the juice. The ringing in her ears slowly died down so she could hear again. He smiled when she placed the empty glass on the table.

He'd changed into a wolf.

That was actually...extraordinary. Totally amazing. Incredible and frightening at the same time.

"So this thing you plan on telling me is that in your secret life you're a pet wolf?"

He burst out laughing, then stopped abruptly. "Sorry, but oh my God, that's funny. No, I am a wolf, but *not* a pet. I mean, I'm a wolf and a human, but it's not like the scary 'moonlight makes me mad and I rip out throats' or anything. Really."

Pam resisted clutching her legs. "Werewolf?"

TJ tilted his head from side to side. "Kinda? But more like I'm a human and I can also change into a wolf. There's no in-between stage."

She shivered involuntarily. He leaned forward as if he planned to come and join her, and she held up a hand. "Don't. Just...don't push it too fast, okay? I think I might be past the point I'm going to fall into a dead faint, but you need to give me some time."

He sat back and folded his hands in his lap, the hopeful expression he wore making her snort. She rose and paced to the door.

"You're not leaving, are you?" He sounded panicked, and she took pity on him. She'd never figure this out if she ran.

"No, but I need to move. Tell me more."

"Okay, except...there isn't much more to tell. I can change into a wolf. Always have been able to, since I was about twelve. Umm, there's a whole bunch of us, and we—"

Oh my God. "Maggie. Does she know about this?"

TJ hesitated. "Pam, I'm going to be completely honest with you, but you have to promise not to freak out."

A laugh escaped—a little thin and quivery around the edges. "I don't think I can promise that, but I'll try."

"Maggie knows. She's always known because she's also a wolf. She married a wolf. My brother is a wolf. His wife is a wolf. Heck, ninety percent of Haines have the wolf gene, either full blood or half. Together we belong to the Granite Lake pack, and we've got a kind of government and hierarchy and, well, it's complicated at times, but usually it's pretty cool."

Pam stopped her pacing and leaned on the wall for a minute to calm herself. Everything she'd ever known as reality was slipping away and somehow she had to make sense of it.

Her best friend was able to change into a wolf and never told her? The huge gorgeous men she'd seen at the wedding were all wolf shifters? Unbelievable, and yet it had to be true. Pain swelled inside, not so much fear, but a lack of certainty. Sadness at what she thought was truth being ripped away.

She turned to TJ. Concern was written all over him, in the tightness of his shoulders, the expression on his face. He shook his head slowly.

"I'm sorry. I didn't want to hurt you like this. Please, *please* don't be scared. I'll do anything in my power to make it better. Anything. Ask as many questions as you want, I swear I'll tell you everything. The only thing I won't do is let anyone harm my family." He stood slowly and held out his arms.

Insane. From one moment to the next she was doing everything wrong. He kidnapped her, and she laughed and had sex with him. Now he revealed he was a wild beast at times, and she was powerless to stop herself from stepping into his arms and accepting his embrace.

She clutched him hard, wrapping her arms around his torso and resting her head on his chest. He rubbed her back in slow, even circles. Under her ear his heart thumped, the consistent pulse reassuring and steady. He didn't say anything—just let her soak in his warmth, the comfort of his presence.

In the midst of her rocking world, he gave her balance.

She drew a deep breath, unsteady and ragged, and he swore. "You're killing me. It's going to be okay. Please, trust me. Nothing bad will happen to you. I'll make sure everything works out." He lifted her chin and stared at her with compassion, his pupils huge.

She tried to smile. "It's getting easier to accept, but I am so going to kick Maggie's butt the next time I see her."

He leaned toward her, his intentions clear, and she held her breath. Did she want to kiss him?

"Pam?"

More than wanted to, needed to. She lifted her mouth and he kissed her carefully. With a gentle stroke he brushed away the tears that had filled her eyes as her world was thrown into chaos.

He traced a finger down her cheek. "Maggie has a story, but it's hers to share, not mine. I will tell you she's always said you were her best friend in the whole world and she loves you a ton. She never kept secrets to hurt you."

She nodded. "Any other bombs you need to drop on me? Like is drinking the Yukon water going to make me able to shift or anything?"

Pain flashed across his face.

"No, afraid it doesn't work that way." He kissed her forehead. "Unfortunately there is one more thing I need to tell you, and it's probably going to be another doozy of a revelation. You want it before or after supper?"

He released her and she went to the sink to splash her face with water. More mysteries? Her heart couldn't take much more.

"Is it really important?"

He nodded. "You should sit down."

Oh shit. "That bad, eh?"

"I'll promise to turn into my wolf afterward and you can twist my ear again if it makes you feel better."

She chuckled. "Goof."

He sighed mightily. "Hold on to your sense of humour, you might need it."

She sat and he sank to the floor at her feet. His expression was serious and concerned, so different than what she'd seen in him over the past days.

"Hey, where's that lighthearted guy who makes me smile gone? You can turn into a wolf. It's not the end of the world, not unless you give me fleas. I hate having to deal with flea infestations."

He took her hands in his and brought them to his lips, kissing her knuckles tenderly.

"No fleas...but something a little more permanent. I mentioned we've got a kind of government? My big brother, Keil, is the head of the Granite Lake pack."

"Really? That's kinda cool. Why is that an issue?"

"Well, it's not, but he's the Alpha since he's the strongest wolf around. There're these unspoken rules that happen in a pack, based on our wolves. Keil and his wife, Robyn, you remember her? They're the top of the heap. Well, one of the other things our wolves decide is..."

He shook his head slowly and brought her hand to his ear. "Here. You may as well grab on now."

How could she stay angry around him? She laughed and leaned forward to give him a kiss, smoothing her fingers through his hair. The sensation distracted her. "That's what your hair reminded me of."

"What?"

She stroked again, reveling in the softness. So soothing to the touch. Something about caressing, being close to TJ made her happy inside, lighting all the dark corners. "Your fur. The night you slept with me in your wolf form I fell asleep stroking you. That's what your hair feels like. So soft."

He shivered. "God, you keep touching me like that and I'm never going to get this out."

She stilled her hands. "Just tell me. It's not like you're going to shock the daylights out of me."

"We're mates."

She paused. "Sure. We're best buds. Whatever you say. Now tell me the rest of the news because getting freaked out seems to have made me hungry."

He shook his head wildly. "No, you don't understand. Mates, as in the way a wolf takes a mate. You know dogs, you must know a little bit about wolves. We have a lot of the characteristics of wolves, and just like there's an alpha and an omega wolf, our wolves pick our mate and they pick them for life. You, me. My wolf picked you."

TJ STARED INTO THE FIRE. It was far too early to be getting up and way too late to still be awake. After his little life-changing revelation, Pam had snatched together the fixings for a sandwich then retreated to the bedroom to "get some space to think". He'd settled in to wait and see what the verdict would be.

He'd screwed everything up. Everything.

Crap, why had he imagined, even for a moment, that hauling Pam into the bush against her will would make anything easier?

Time alone, right. He poked the logs and watched the sparks fly upward in protest. That's what he had now, time *completely* alone. Just him and the couch, which was lumpy and uncomfortable, and he'd sleep on it for the next week without a single complaint if Pam would give them a chance.

He'd sleep on it forever if she asked him to.

The floorboards creaked in the bedroom and he stood in a rush, staring at the door in the hopes she'd come out. The freaky part was he could sense where she was—and what she was feeling—just a little. His brother had explained once how the connection between him and his mate Robyn worked. While this wasn't as strong as Keil had described, it was vivid enough to give TJ a teeny tiny fraction of hope to cling to.

Maybe there would be more to their mate connection than he'd dreamed possible.

When she'd barricaded herself in the bedroom, she'd been royally pissed at him, and he'd taken it in stride. It was the confusion that followed and the tears shortly after that had him on the verge of ignoring her request and breaking down the door, because he knew he could comfort her.

Needed to comfort her.

Now he stood as still as possible, trying to figure out a way to connect with her. They had made love—it had to count for something. In spite of the damn condom, there *had* to be a bond to help them make it through this rough beginning.

She wasn't sleeping, and she wasn't mad. An even calm greeted him, and now he was the one confused.

Calm? After all he'd thrown at her in the past couple days?

Holy shit, she was the most intriguing person he'd ever met, and right there in that moment all his doubts washed away.

If he had to turn his back on his family to be with her, so be it. He'd move south, find a job. He'd still have to turn wolf every now and then, but he'd find a way to do that wherever she was. He'd court her properly, and eventually she'd accept him, if not as a lover, then as a friend.

It would kill a part of him, but being with her would be worth it.

The door creaked open an inch and their eyes met. He bit his lip. *Let her call the shots.* Her lashes were still wet from her earlier tears and something tore at his belly. His resolve wavered.

Okay, not comforting his mate? Sucked donkey balls.

"Can we talk?"

TJ nodded so rapidly his vision blurred. Pam opened the door wider. He hauled his gaze off where the oversized T-shirt she wore barely covered the tops of her thighs. This was not the time to get distracted, even though his mate made his knees weak with longing.

"Here's the deal. I know you're not lying about being a wolf. I saw it."

Promising opening.

"I also believe you're insane, in the nicest possible way."

Umm, that doesn't sound as good. Begging commences now… "Tell me what you want me to do that would fix this for you. If you want, I'll shift to my wolf and run until I find a place with a phone. It will take me a while to organize, but I'm sure I can find a way to get you home early."

She snorted. "You're not getting out of this that easy, buster." Pam stalked to his side and grabbed him by the collar. She eyed him up and down and his fading hope flickered back to life. "You promised me seven days of wilderness adventures, with lots of hot monkey sex thrown in."

"What are you saying?" He could barely breathe.

"Well, other than you have to offer hot *wolfie* sex, I'm making you stick to your commitment. But you've now got an additional challenge. You say we're 'mates'. Fine. You have until the end of the week to prove it."

8

———

The past couple of hours had been sheer agony as Pam fought with herself to pick the right thing to do next.

Step one: get abducted by a virtual stranger? *Check.*

Two: completely forget all rules of safety and have sex with said kidnapper? *Check.*

Three: have the guy she was developing suspiciously strong feelings for turn into a wild animal in front of her then suggest they were meant to be together for the rest of their lives? Once you put a check in that box, what the hell were you supposed to do for a follow-up performance?

But it was true. She'd seen him change—it was a reality she had to face, no matter how much her mind rebelled at the thought. Shrieking or wailing wouldn't move this situation forward.

Logic was always the best thing to fall back on. Logic, and an oversized baseball bat.

TJ rocked on his feet, his hands twisting together until he deliberately shoved them into his pockets. "You don't want me to get us back to Haines?"

She shook her head. "If we go back now that doesn't answer any more of my questions, does it? I suspect once we reach civilization we're going to have a few other issues to deal with."

TJ's cringe said it all. Yup—that hierarchy he'd mentioned in passing—she bet he was up the creek without a paddle in their books right now.

His big brother was in charge? Thinking back to the way the whole group had worked her at the wedding ceremony, she suspected there were a few well-greased wheels in play. Who knew what weird rules TJ had broken? Someone was undoubtedly on the lookout for them even now.

But this was *her* life and she would be the one to make the decisions. Not some well-meaning older brother, or even Maggie, although Pam suspected her BFF could answer a few questions.

In spite of the adrenaline rush that had spiked through her for most of the evening and night, or maybe because of it, an enormous yawn overtook her.

TJ spoke quietly. "Let's call it a night and tomorrow I'll do my best to show you...well, I'll show you how this works. But anytime you have questions, you ask. I promise I won't keep anything from you."

"Holding your tongue doesn't seem to be the issue, TJ."

"Sorry, very true."

Pam covered her mouth as another yawn hit her. Bed. It was past two and definitely time for some sleep.

She turned and paced into the bedroom. The chill in the air encouraged her to dive under the quilt. She pounded the pillows a few times trying to settle in comfortably when she realized she was alone. She sat up to see TJ staring at her from where he still stood in the living room.

"Aren't you coming?"

"You want me to sleep with you?" He dragged a hand through his hair. "Okay. I mean, I want to join you, but..."

He walked forward slowly, dropping into a crouch beside the bed. His long fingers carefully stroked back a strand of hair from her forehead and his touch sent a shiver through her.

"Pam. You want me to prove we're mates, then here's the first demonstration. I think getting into bed with you right now would be a mistake. You're still in shock, and while there's this incredible physical pull between us because we are mates, if anything happens sexually you're going to regret it.

"Still, I can feel how much you need to be comforted right now, and so here's the best I can do."

He kissed her forehead tenderly then walked to the opposite side of the bed. He turned his back and stripped off his shirt, tossing it on a nearby chair.

The pale light from the dying fire leaked in through the open doorway, brushing delicate highlights along the solid ridges of his body. Pam sucked for air. He was simply gorgeous. The way he moved made her hot and bothered, even when he wasn't turning sexual attention on her.

There was a huge grin on his face as he pivoted and sank to his knees. "The way you're looking at me is giving me a thrill. I'll shift back when you need me in the morning."

Though she watched as carefully as possible, she couldn't figure out how he did it. One minute he was a human, stooping low to the ground, the next a beautiful wolf leapt onto the bed beside her. He batted her with his head, blowing warm air from his nostrils as he nuzzled her neck.

Something simply amazing—followed by something normal. It was so TJ. "Goof."

He licked her cheek from jawbone to temple, a long slow drag that made her giggle. As one they settled, her arms wrapped around him, her fingers tangled in his fur to hold him close.

A tight ball of fear she'd been denying slipped out from inside her belly and unraveled.

How had he known? She'd needed to take charge and make this work. And yeah, she had the major hots for him. But this? She stroked his fur and he let loose a rumble, soft and low, in his throat. He radiated calmness, cautiously rolling to avoid bumping her too hard.

Closing her eyes, she was surrounded by a strong sensation of peace. His rhythmic heartbeat felt perfect under her hands as she fell asleep stroking him.

TJ WAS STILL in wolf form when they woke, and his enthusiastic good-morning kisses made her laugh until her stomach hurt. Her heart ached a little since that's how Damon used to greet her—with a wet tongue-lashing that had her scrambling for cover as he chased her around the tangled bed sheets.

Damn it, her new boyfriend reminded her of her dog. This couldn't be good.

She pushed him back enough she could sit up. He rested his chin on her thigh, big beautiful eyes staring up unblinking. She'd slept like a rock, his warm furry body pressed against her side, comforting and reassuring.

"Good morning, TJ."

He tilted his head to the side, his eyes sparkling at her. One ear wiggled and she swore he sighed with contentment. Damn, he was cute. "Dibs on the shower, then you can tell me what you've got planned for today."

TJ jumped off the bed and headed out the open door, leaving her alone in the room. She stripped off her sleep shirt and grabbed her things.

Mates. Werewolves. The calm, contented feeling she'd woken to dissipated a little. How come she hadn't screamed and run away after waking up with a wolf in her bed?

Because it felt right?

The shower wasn't hot enough to wash away the rest of her unease, no matter how long she stayed in. Still, she'd offered TJ time to prove his point. Not that she had much choice about getting out of the wilderness without his help.

When her fingers and toes grew wrinkled, she abandoned the water to face what the day would hold.

She rubbed a towel over her hair as she joined him at the kitchen table.

The toasted bagels were only slightly burnt. A fully human TJ poured her a cup of coffee and passed her the sugar container, his damp hair sticking up in spikes.

"Where did you shower?"

He pointed out the window. "In the lake."

Pam shivered. "You're kidding. The water is freezing."

"It's too cold for me in my human form, but my wolf doesn't mind a bit."

She took a long pull at her coffee, letting the heat of it wash over her. It may be a handy solution—having two forms like that—but she was grateful it had been him in the lake and not her.

He handed her a note pad. "We've all got in the habit of carrying paper around for those times we need to talk with Robyn and our sign language isn't adequate. While you were showering, I jotted down a few notes to distract me."

"Distract you?"

His gaze rolled down one side of her and up the other, and suddenly the room grew a whole lot warmer. "You were naked in the shower. Imagining you in there..."

Their eyes met and Pam swallowed around the bit of bagel stuck in her throat. Oh lordy, what had she gotten herself into? She stared at him, the dark pools of his eyes enticing her to dive in.

He nudged the notepad and broke the connection. "As per orders, I've got adventure activities planned for each day, but I've added to them. This list is the things that are normal for wolf mates to experience around each other. I thought we could work our way through some of them—sort of see how things go, and still get in the activities you signed up for originally."

He leaned forward and took her hand, his expression shifting from flirtatious to contrite. "I want to say one more time I'm really sorry I didn't ask you straight out if you wanted to get involved with me. I should have done things differently."

Wow. An unasked-for apology from a guy? Pam sat for a minute not sure what to say. "Okay."

She glanced at the paper. He'd drawn five circles on the page, overlapping them in the middle like a malformed daisy. Paired words filled each circle.

Mental link

Chemical attraction

Physical connection

Emotional attachment

Complementary interests

Pam hesitated. He was taking this damn seriously. "Chemical attraction? Isn't that the same thing as physical connection?"

TJ shook his head. "Not at all. One leads to the other, but I can assure you they are very different." He brushed the back of his knuckles against her cheek before tucking her hair behind her ear. "This one might be hard to prove—heck they're all going to be tough, but this one might be the most wolfish. I'm guessing a bit, since I only know what I've been told about wolves' experiences. You being human..." He shrugged.

"So you don't know exactly what you're trying to prove?"

His eyes flashed. "Oh, I know exactly what I'm going to prove. That you and I belong together, without any doubt whatsoever."

Pam pushed back her chair slightly, feeling caged by his intensity. She grabbed the notepad and held it between them, dragging air into her lungs to calm the blood racing through her.

"Okay, chemical. In short that means? What?"

TJ took a slow, deep inhalation and moaned. "I am never going to be able to do that without getting hard. Okay— what it means is you smell right. I'm not talking about your perfume or your soap, but you." He closed his eyes and gripped the table tightly. "Just the smell of you makes me go weak-kneed. It makes me want to pick you up, carry you to bed and make love to you for hours."

Pam shivered, erotic images flashing in her mind.

He opened his eyes. "But it also makes me want to sit beside you for hours and listen to you tell me about your favourite food, and your day at work, and stories about when you were growing up."

Her stomach clenched before she deliberately relaxed it. No way he wanted to hear that kind of crap.

"So it's different from seeing someone at a bar or a dance club and getting turned on? Or for that matter, watching Chris Pine in a movie and feeling the dire need to jump him?"

He rolled his eyes. "What is it with you chicks and that guy? No, not quite the same thing. More like—what would you do if you met him in person?"

She laughed. "Probably freeze."

"Right, and when we met, you wanted to...?"

She thought back to before the wedding. To the almost overwhelming desire to get to know him more intimately. "So we like how each other smells. I don't know if that's enough to prove anything to me."

TJ sat back and sipped his juice. "As long as you agree there is something—magnetic—between us."

She nodded slowly. That much she would confess to. It would also explain why no matter what insane thing he did, she responded the wrong way.

TJ tugged the notepad from her fingers. "Eat, the day is wasting. That's not the item on our agenda for today anyway."

Pam blinked in surprise. "It's not?"

"Nope." He topped up her coffee and raised his mug in a toast. "To working our way through the mate list."

HIDE AND GO SEEK. She was playing hide and go seek in the Yukon bush with a werewolf. Pam tucked her legs a little closer to her body and made sure nothing was sticking out.

They'd spent the morning hiking to an abandoned miner's cabin and poking around for artifacts. After lunch he'd casually proposed this game, and now she sat in the branches of a tree, her body pressed against the trunk. TJ walked straight toward her like she'd left a trail of breadcrumbs for him to follow. He grinned at her and held out a hand.

"You need to work harder at this or I'm going to think you're not trying."

"You're cheating. You've got lupine senses, don't you, even in your human form?" There had to be a reason he'd found her so quickly. The last *five* times she'd hidden.

TJ shook his head. "Well, I can smell you, but I can also feel where you are. It's like I told you, there's a mental link between us, and I'm following that." She pushed off the branch and he caught her, her body settling against his, warm and comfortable as she wrapped her arms around his neck.

"Fine. You can find me in a snowstorm. That's a cool trick."

"Hey, don't think this is a one-way street. I think you'll be able to do it as well."

He placed her on the grassy area outside the cabin yet refused to let her out of his arms.

"You planning on proving the physical connection right now?"

He flashed a grin. "No, but you wait. When we get kinky in bed, I'll know what you want. How hard, how fast." One hand skimmed her shoulder and down her spine, coming to rest on the small of her back. Intimate. The airy touch of his caress sent a tingling sensation racing up her body and her nipples tightened involuntarily. TJ spoke, his voice deep and husky. "Of course that means I can totally tease you."

Oh my God, do it now. The need to offer herself up on a silver platter was instinctive, and somewhat frightening. Time to retreat. She pressed her hands to his chest to separate them enough she could think. "Two-way street, bud? Be careful there, I might have to write you out a ticket."

He cupped her chin with his free hand. His grasp firmed until she lifted her gaze to meet his. "Don't. Don't hide behind jokes right now."

Pam closed her eyes and waited. His warm breath caressed her cheek as he brought their bodies back in contact.

"You look beautiful in the sunlight."

She opened her eyes just as he brushed his lips against hers. His dark lashes fluttered against her skin. She stroked her tongue into his mouth, no longer fighting the delightful sensations that streaked through her body.

They stood there, kissing slowly, hands gently exploring each other's bodies—Pam lost all track of time and slipped into a dreamy place where there were no issues hanging over her head. No need to discover if fairytales really could come true.

When they pulled apart, his smile warmed her through and through. "Well, that's not what I had planned, but I'll certainly take it. Stop distracting me. Your turn to hunt. No peeking while I hide."

Pam not only closed her eyes, she covered her face with her hands, like a child afraid they would be tempted to cheat. She didn't want to have any clue which direction he was headed. No chance she could pretend this was a fair test when it wasn't. She hummed quietly to cover any accidental sounds he might make that would give her a direction to head. Inspiration hit and she counted out loud.

"...ten, eleven, twelve...I hope you're hiding well because if I find you standing out in the open somewhere you have to buy me a crab dinner or something....seventeen, eighteen... or a case of beer, I could really go for a cold drink...twenty-three, twenty-four, twenty-five...ready or not, you must be caught."

She opened her eyes and took a long look around. The sun sparkled on the surface of the lake across from her, the tiny ripples from the whispering breeze creating a kaleidoscope of colour and light.

Out by the cabin, the porch swing shifted slowly and she watched for a moment, but it sped up, didn't slow. The wind again, not TJ brushing it. She examined the bush, but other than natural shaking and trembling in the leaves she could see no clear hint of where TJ was hiding.

"Okay, I'll give you this much, you've hidden well. Now..."

The usual procedure would be to divide the area into sectors and methodically work her way through them. She paused. This wasn't supposed to be like a usual search, right? If they were mates, she should be able to sense him.

She sniffed the air then laughed. No, she wasn't the one with the wolf nose.

Pam was still chuckling when she felt it. Almost a...lightness in the air, a sense of emotion brushing past her. TJ was pleased. Admiring her?

She pressed a hand to her chest. It wasn't just her imagination. She closed her eyes once more and covered her ears. The wind in the trees faded away and all sound stilled, but the sensation increased. Oh my God, she *could* feel something.

She twirled and ran for the cabin. The pounding of her footfalls as she raced up the stairs echoed off the low roof and she jerked open the door.

Disappointment hit her hard. She'd fully expected to find TJ on the couch. She'd felt sure he was there. Sitting comfortably, waiting for her.

Again, a tug. Like strings attached inside her heart.

She paced the cabin in confusion. He was supposed to be here.

"TJ, where *are* you?"

The sensation refused to go away. She checked under the bed, in the shower stall. Stepping outside, she kicked a rock in frustration before a flash of inspiration made her curse.

"You turkey." She raced around the back of the cabin to where the woodpile was stacked into a rough façade of a staircase. She scrambled to the top where it was level with the lightly inclined roof of the attached storage lean-to, and stared at TJ. He lay flat on his back on a thick blanket, grinning at her.

"Hey."

Deep satisfaction stole over her as she cautiously made her way to his side. "Hey, yourself. You got up here pretty damn quick."

His shit-eating grin grew larger. "And it took you oh-so-long to find me, didn't it?"

Holy crap, he was right. In the midst of the hunt, she'd lost grasp of the fact she had found him. Had known where he was. "Wow."

TJ patted the blanket. "How did you do it?"

Pam settled next to him, nestling into his arms. "I'm not completely sure. It's like I knew. But, it's not possible…"

He nuzzled at her temple. "Hmm, you just proved it is." His lips descended slowly to press, warm and soft, against her jawbone. He snuck his fingers into her hair and brought their mouths together, and she couldn't be bothered to try to figure out why she'd known where he was. She'd known. Score one for the mating list. Bring on the sex.

She rolled him and crawled on top, keeping their mouths together. His tongue was doing this intricate dance inside her mouth that made the hair on the back of her neck stand upright. She took her revenge by lowering her hips onto his groin. TJ countered with a move that slid both his hands up her torso to cup her breasts and suddenly she hated Wonderbra with a passion.

One motion stripped off her T-shirt. Another released her from the confining bra and TJ growled.

"Oh yes." He pulled her closer, catching hold of one nipple between his teeth. His fingers stroked her ribs, making her skin come alive as he sucked, switching from side to side. The slight breeze whispered past her wet nipples and they tightened even more. All around the gentle noises of nature carried on—birds chirping, the leaves rustling in an uneven beat. The slurps and moans and small cries of passion escaping their lips fit perfectly in the mix, and Pam thought she'd never been in a more beautiful place.

She pulled away to gaze at him, his ever-present smile warming her heart, the lust and passion on his face heating her soul. "As fun as this is, I don't think the roof is a good place to make love."

His eyes widened and he lunged upward to mesh their bodies together once more, and suddenly she found herself flat on her back under him. The blanket protected her from the ridges of the roof shingles and the sun broke out in full glory.

The light in his eyes outshone it.

"I think anywhere is a fabulous place to make love to you."

Her heart skipped a beat. Then she couldn't see his face anymore as he dropped toward her, his lips doing wicked things to her torso, his fingers playing her body as skillfully as he played his guitar.

Oh yeah, he was talented. The simmer of desire in her belly bloomed, and oddly the roof of the cabin seemed a lovely place for a little sexual jaunt. Only...

"Did you bring a condom?" Even the question came out sounding like *fuck me now*. Breathless, needy. Lustful.

He rose over her. "We don't need one, you know. I won't carry any STDs since shifting to my wolf heals almost everything germ or virus related."

"Almost?"

The heavy weight of his groin pressed against her center as he nestled between her thighs, and it felt so good a little bit of her brain melted.

"The common cold still sucks."

Oh Lord, he kissed her again—kisses that were far too distracting. Far too enticing as he rocked their hips together intimately. The fabric separating them was a lifesaver and she wiggled under him. Sex was out unless they crawled off each other for long enough to gain the cabin. Still, there was no reason they couldn't find satisfaction.

"Let me up."

He rolled off, disappointment written all over him. Until she stripped off her shorts and reached for his zipper.

"Are we going to...?"

"No." She manhandled him to his back and yanked off his pants. "We're not having sex without a condom. I'm sorry, what you said makes sense, but I can't just accept your word on something as big as that."

He lay back and threw an arm across his eyes, his chest heaving. His erection stood straight from his groin. Hmm. The sexual hum in her body hit deafening levels so she reached out and grasped him firmly.

"Holy fuck." He thrust into her hand and she laughed.

"I'm no tease. We can go inside and grab a condom for round two. Right now…" Pam stroked him, her fingers passing lightly over the head of his erection to gather the moisture leaking from the tip. With her palm wet, it was easy to slide along his length, each pass drawing a groan of pleasure from his lips. The sunlight shone on them and she drew in a deep breath of the crisp air. The scent of their bodies rose around them and made her happy inside.

Everything about TJ made her happy inside, if she was honest.

His hands grasped her hips and lifted her.

"What are you doing?" She let go of his cock and threw out her hands to catch herself. A second later she was on hands and knees, palms resting on the blanket on either side of his hips. She followed the line of his body to where his head nestled between her knees. He licked his lips and her sex pulsed.

"You use your hands, but I get to use my mouth."

Yee-ha.

He tugged her backward and suddenly the fact they were on a roof vanished. The need to discover if they were mates? Out the proverbial window because the guy had a magical tongue and he was using it to her utmost advantage. He licked—light teasing touches, followed by full-out forceful sweeps from the sensitive skin near her anus to the apex of her mound.

Nibbles on her labia. Sucking her clit. She rocked back in an attempt to get him closer but his grip on her hips held her fast. He was in control and there was nothing she could do to change that fact.

Except distract him. She glanced at his cock and planned her counterattack. One hand on the roof to balance, one hand to wrap around him and pump.

The reverberation of his groan against her nether lips sent an electric shock racing. Fireworks zapped past her nipples and looped back to ignite the fuse in her core. He gripped her ass tighter, massaging and squeezing her cheeks as he ground her down on his face. His hot wet tongue slid into her, and it was so incredible she stopped moving for a second. Let the sensations build until she trembled on the verge of release. The euphoria took her so high that when he thrust two fingers deep into her core and sucked her clit hard, it was all over. Blood pounded past her ears and her head spun.

It took a while until the waves slowed enough she could think again.

TJ lapped slowly, his touch more and more gentle until she let him help her shift to snuggle against his side. His thick cock pressed her hip and she took a deep breath, guilt haunting her.

"That was selfish of me."

TJ possessed her mouth for a long breathless kiss. The taste of her pleasure on his lips made her shiver.

He pulled away and touched their foreheads together. "Not selfish. Timing is everything. You needed to concentrate, and I wanted to give to you." He tugged her fingers to his lips and kissed her knuckles, and something in her heart tightened a little. What had he said about a physical connection? She rarely came from oral sex if she was giving at the same time.

Her finger was surrounded by wet heat as he sucked the digit into his mouth. One by one he wet them before placing her hand on his erection and wrapping his fingers over hers. "Now it's my turn, and you can give to me."

Tip to root he guided her, increasing the pressure. His lips found hers again, and their tongues slid together sensually as the stroke-stroke continued. Not too fast, but solid. Firm.

Pam dug her fingers into his hair and tugged his head back, exposing his throat. He let her kiss her way down. She paused, breathing deeply with her face buried in his neck before licking back up, the salty taste of him like a fine wine. He filled her senses—the touch of their skin so wicked and sensual. The sound of their joint hands an erotic contrast with the delicate sounds of nature.

He tightened under her hand and with a groan he came. The hot fluid of his seed coated their hands and sprayed out farther to land willy-nilly between their naked torsos.

They sat together until their hearts stopped thumping, warmth radiating out from TJ like a space heater. Pam nestled closer and pressed their chests together, heedless of the moisture on their skin.

"That was pretty awesome, if I do say so."

TJ grinned. "How about a shower before a little more awesome? I think we can work it into the schedule."

The schedule was getting better all the time. "Deal."

She grabbed their clothes into a pile and he protested mildly. "You want us to crawl down naked?"

Pam reached out a hand toward him, dragging a finger through the moisture clinging to his firm abdomen. "I'm not putting clothes on a sticky body for five minutes when they have to last us a week."

TJ shrugged, then picked up the blanket. She made her way cautiously to the edge of the roof and threw the clothes to the ground. TJ held her hand as she slipped a foot over to find the precarious top of the woodpile. Heading down wasn't as easy as she remembered the upward journey had been.

"I can't believe I actually raced up here."

Once both feet were down, one log wobbled underfoot and she grasped TJ to regain her balance. She took her time, testing each step until she made it to the bottom safely.

He copied her and threw down the blanket then spun around to place his feet. *Hmm, what a nice ass.*

He descended a few steps, and she was just thinking how nicely the front view complimented the back when a loud crack rang out. The logs under his feet rolled and bucked, and suddenly TJ was fast approaching the ground, almost surfing the pile of timber that had seemingly come to life.

Individual logs shook and spun, some falling to the side, some twisting in place as the entire mound collapsed. The wood crackled and snapped with an alarming volume, the clatter echoing off the cabin wall. Random logs fell left and right as he twirled his arms to maintain balance. Pam stepped out of the path of danger, watching with dread as the stack disintegrated.

The once neat load completed its tumble to the ground, one final log teetering for a second before joining the rest with a gentle *plop*, TJ askew on top of the messy heap.

9

—————

TJ lay face down on the mattress, sure his face was as red as his butt. Stabbing pain shot through his right ass cheek, and he pressed up on his elbows with a curse.

"Damn it all, leave them. They'll fall out eventually. Ouch, shit. Stop it."

Pam laughed as she applied the tweezers again, trying to remove a few more of the splinters he'd gained upon contact with the firewood. "Stop being a whiny puppy."

He growled and her laughter grew louder. He collapsed and grit his teeth together. *Fuck*, it felt like she was digging post holes. "You having fun back there?"

"Uh-huh."

Shit. He cringed again at an especially hard spike. "Bet you sucked at playing Operation when you were little."

Pam gave an extra deep dig. "Horrible. Lost every time."

He buried his face in the pillow and bit it. Hard.

She giggled. An honest to God, full-out girlish giggle that ended in a snort and TJ couldn't take it anymore. He whirled, captured her in his arms and dragged her under him.

"Hey, I haven't got them all yet." She tangled her hands in his hair and pressed their mouths together, and all the splinters in the world weren't enough to distract him from finding a condom and pleasing his mate all over again.

And again. On the bed, in the shower. Heck, they barely got supper cooking before his wolf prompted him to press her to the tabletop and take her from behind. The fragrant aroma of tomato sauce filled the cabin, the water for the spaghetti noodles boiled unminded in the pot as he pounded into her.

Pam's shouts of encouragement took them both to the edge quicker than he wanted. Every slide into her body nudged her farther into his heart. She reached back and grabbed his hand, threading their fingers together. He slowed and pressed his front to her back, twisting her head to the side to be able to stare into her eyes.

"This is real, Pam." He thrust forward slowly, gazes locked together. "You, me. Together like this."

She tightened her fingers.

Another rock of his hips. Another time being squeezed by her body so tight he could barely breathe. But it was the expression in her eyes that took his breath away.

So much hope, and so much fear. His wolf howled and he fought back the urge to claim her completely. Beat down the desire to take charge before she was ready. TJ closed his eyes and held on to control with a fine thread. All the while, they moved together.

It was probably the only thing that saved him. Pam's willing presses against him as she rose to meet his thrusts calmed his wolf. Gave him the chance to ease the beast back and return to his human control once more. He tucked one hand around her torso, one hand between her legs to help her along, rubbing her clit in time with their joining until he felt her tighten under him, her orgasm grasping him in waves. He buried himself in her and let his restraints go, wishing with all his heart she was ready to accept all of him.

Forever.

~

"ANOTHER LIST?"

TJ took another couple of slow paddles, directing their canoe toward the bay they had selected. Day four, and time was slipping away too rapidly. The afternoon sun sparkled around them, the setting as idyllic as any picture postcard, but he felt a sense of urgency he'd never had before in the wilderness. Proving they were mates was like proving to a child the sun would rise in the morning. Facts could only explain so much before you had to let go and trust. "You can put your paddle away and I'll let you take a peek. Oh, and you can turn around. I'm going to drop anchor while we fish."

Pam tucked away the paddle and carefully lifted her legs over the gunwales as she rotated. The long line of bare skin showing below the edge of her shorts made his mouth water, and he stared off into the bush and thought of nasty things to divert his mind.

When the canoe stopped rocking he checked to make sure she was seated comfortably, then passed over the papers he had stashed in his pocket. She unfolded them and smoothed the creases. "The mate list. Which one are we going to do today?"

"Complementary interests."

She stared at the paper and he wondered why she looked so sad. Why the burst of pleasure he felt from her faded so quickly to something close to despair. His connection with her had leveled out over the past two days, and he doubted it would grow any stronger until they actually made love without protection and he marked her as his. What they had now was like a shadow reflecting the real connection he considered possible. It was there, undeniable to him, but he ached for more.

Pam put on a happy face and refolded the paper, tucking it into her back pocket. She glanced at the second sheet of paper still lying in her lap and laughed. "Oh my God, are you expecting me to write an essay or something? I'm on holidays. I'm not into reports right now."

"Hell no, those are topics to discuss. See, most mates I know have common interests. Robyn and Keil, you should see them on the slopes. They're both totally insane skiers when they're not leading a group. Erik and Maggie are both classical literature buffs."

"So you think we should have a bunch of interests in common?"

She settled into the bottom of the canoe and adjusted her lifejacket so she could lean back on the front seat and use it as a backrest. Her long legs stretched out into the center of the craft, and TJ eyed them with longing. He sighed. No. While he'd been more fortunate than usual with his clumsiness so far this week, fooling around in a canoe would not end up a pretty picture.

"TJ?"

He caught her eye and stumbled for words. "I was staring again, wasn't I?"

She blushed lightly, then tossed her head back, her dark hair bouncing around her shoulders. "I don't mind. But back to the question..."

"I think we could have things in common, or we could be like Tad and Missy—they often have interests that when you put them together you get something that fits. He makes things out of wood and she enjoys sewing. Together they've made all kinds of gifts for the pack, like baby cradles and receiving blankets, and decorative wall quilts and hangers to display them on."

Pam nodded slowly. "They complete each other. You think we're going to have matches like that?"

"Over the past couple days as we've talked I think I've heard a few things, but I don't want to skew the results and use those as an example. So you pick one item, think of an answer but before you tell me what you would say, I'll share mine."

She grinned as she examined the paper. "This could be fun you know."

Her mischief-maker persona was back. God, he loved it when her eyes got all sparkly and her face lit up. It made it easier to breath. Made the whole of his soul content.

He baited the hooks, added a bobber and cast out the line, passing the first rod to her before setting up his own. Fishing was a great opportunity for long conversations.

Pam ran a finger down the list before glancing at him, an innocent expression plastered to her face. *Not.* "Okay—what's your favourite sport for exercise?"

Easy. "Running." Mostly as a wolf, but that still counted.

She snorted. "Mine is baseball. Well, that one works, we can play fetch together, right?"

He flicked water at her and the boat rocked lightly as she laughed.

"Number two. Favourite thing to do to relax?"

TJ gripped the fishing rod firmly in lieu of reaching for her. "My new response would be to make love with you, but before this week I would have said make music."

The flash of desire in her eyes was unmistakable. "Stop."

They stared at each other. Her pulse pounded in the hollow of her throat and he ached. "What's your answer, Pam?"

She licked her lips. "I was going to say listen to music."

Yup, she could try to deny it, but there was more and more evidence to prove they were meant to be together.

Her fishing rod quivered and she scrambled upright, the paper falling unminded to the bottom of the canoe. He laughingly coached her through reeling in the fish. For the next two hours they floated and fished, releasing all but one of the rainbow trout while they worked their way through the entire list he'd prepared. By now the paper was wet and smelled like fish, and when the time came to turn the canoe back toward the dock, Pam had nothing but content emotions streaming from her.

"You relax, I'll get us home." He paddled hard, eyes on the water occasionally. Most of the time his gaze caressed her body where she leaned back, arms resting easily on the gunwales as she glanced around at the nearby mountains.

"I can't believe someone gets to live here for more than a holiday."

"The summers are fabulous, but in a remote location like this they don't stay all winter, and winter comes early in the North. My friends usually use this cabin from May to August, then they have a place farther south for the rest of the year."

He stroked evenly, wondering why it was far harder than usual to keep the canoe headed in a straight line. It was too clichéd to think looking at her made him weak with desire.

"When does the helicopter return for us?" Her eyes were closed as she spoke, the lazy contentment still emanating from her. TJ relaxed from the instant alert her question had raised.

"Around two o'clock, three days from now. We'll get dropped off in Haines, and we'll have to get a lift back to Maggie and Erik's. The tour you were supposed to take will be done by noon."

She laughed and leaned forward to wrap her arms around her knees. Her dark eyes sparkled at him. "Thank you."

"For what?"

Pam pointed around. "For this. I know we've still got unanswered questions between the two of us, but I wouldn't give up this experience for anything. I like this much better, being quiet and remote. It's far more my style than the daily routine of traveling with a tour group."

TJ stuttered for a second in confusion. "You signed up for it. That first day you said I had no right—"

She raised a hand. "I know, I was wrong. I went along with Maggie's suggestion because I didn't see any other possible way to experience the wilderness in a short time. A single female, traveling alone, just isn't smart. You did okay when you kidnapped me. You really did know a little bit about what I truly needed."

"Well, I'm glad you're comfortable with it now."

Her soft smile teased him. "You're comfortable—in a completely unsettling and life-unraveling way."

They laughed together easily and TJ drew in a deep breath of the crisp air. Hope stirred.

He switched paddling sides to give his arm a rest. They were closing in on the dock but he'd never found a canoe to be so awkward and slow to maneuver.

Pam trailed her fingers in the water lazily, ribbons of waves streaming out on either side of her fingers. Three days left to make a difference.

TJ wondered briefly what chaos was happening back in Haines, but he'd pay that piper when he had to. Now they had a rainbow trout to enjoy for supper, and the evening stretched open before them.

From the expression in her eyes she had a few ideas of how they could spend their time, and he'd be a willing participant in anything she planned.

They arrived at the dock and he held firmly to the decking as she scrambled out. All the equipment came out one at a time until he looked around for the anchor.

Pam burst out laughing, gesturing behind the canoe. "Are those greens to accompany the fish for dinner?"

He swung his head to see a huge mess of lake weed gathered behind the boat. "Where did that come from?" He scrambled onto the dock and followed the line of her pointing finger. "Oh shit. No wonder it was so hard to paddle."

Pam lay on her belly on the deck to grab the anchor rope. She pulled, hauling up the weeds and the anchor he'd neglected to bring in, instead trailing it behind them the whole length of the lake.

He sighed. Yup, two steps forward, one step back. At least it was better than tipping them over.

TJ SAT on the steps of the porch, plucking the strings of the old guitar they'd found in the storage closet. Every day since she'd discovered he was a wolf, he'd played for her. She'd grown to anticipate the quiet time to sit and think.

Today more than ever she needed it. Tomorrow would be their last full day together before the helicopter returned. Pam curled up on the porch swing and watched the sunset. They faced the lake straight on, and the glow rising behind the western mountains painted the entire scene in shades of tangerine and gold. Streaks of light shone on them, and she smiled when TJ's dark colouring lightened as a brilliant flash of pink lit his torso.

The gentle tones of the guitar washed over her. She closed her eyes and rocked dreamily, reveling in her situation. A full belly, a glass of wine at her elbow. After-dinner music. Life couldn't get much better.

She had slight aches and pains from the various activities of the past days. True to his word, TJ had let her try out all kinds of outdoor experiences, including a madcap kayak trip down the nearby river.

Also true to his word, some of her aches were from the very frequent and extremely pleasurable hot wolfie sex they'd been enjoying. And for the past day, every time he grabbed a condom from their dwindling supply she'd been close to telling him to forget it...

It was official. She was going mad.

The kidnapping was no longer an issue. They had become good enough friends it was actually kind of difficult to remember this wasn't what she'd signed up for. She had questions that remained, but her lurking suspicion was when the week officially came to an end, she would be reluctant to leave him behind and head south to resume her normal routine.

The change in her mental processes bewildered her.

"That was a big sigh." TJ examined her closely, his dark eyes peering into her soul. "What deep thoughts are making you so sad?"

Shit. The relaxed peace faded a little. There was such a short time left before their ride appeared to return them to civilization, and she still didn't know what to do. "Thinking about everything you've shown me. You know, the mating list and all."

He strummed softly for a minute, the light melody from the finger-picked strings floating around them. He meant to soothe her, she was sure of it, but as the now-familiar tune he played filled her ears and her heart, tears threatened. It was the same song he'd sung to her at the wedding, with eternal love and new hope all tied up in it.

She wanted more and more to believe.

TJ leaned back on the upper porch railing. "There's this older couple who run the Chilkat Bakery in town. Both human. I think they said they've been married for fifty-five years."

Pam glanced at him with suspicion. Where was this going? "So?"

He placed the guitar aside and joined her on the swing. "You ever seen a couple like that? Married for so long, they seem to read each other's minds?" He wrapped a hand around her neck to massage the tight muscles. "They seem to know exactly what the other person needs at any time."

"Are you saying humans can have a mating connection? I've never heard that before in my life."

"Okay, maybe it's not exactly the same thing, but it must be fairly close. I've seen it. They know each other so deeply they anticipate each other's thoughts, and needs. That's what it's like for wolves—the only thing that seems to be different is how quickly it happens. For wolves, it's instant. In humans, I've seen it in couples who have been together for a long time."

Pam bit her lip. *Frick.* Again, him with the logic. She couldn't fight logic, and yet the ball of fear in her belly didn't want to disappear.

"What are your parents like?"

She turned toward him. Yeah, he knew all the right buttons to push, far better than any person she'd met before. Not even Maggie had asked about her family that quickly. "We're divorced."

TJ's face fell. "Shit."

"Yeah."

"Okay, so I guess they're not a great example." He stopped and stared at her for second. "Hang on, what do you mean 'we're divorced'?"

Pam dragged a hand through her hair. "They got divorced when I was about ten, and proceeded to make my life miserable. They both screwed up holiday plans to get revenge on the other. They fought over me like a dog with a bone, but when they had time with me they ignored me, or seemed to begrudge the fact they had to expend energy on my stuff."

"By the time I was sixteen I'd had enough. I divorced them and went to live with my gramma who was completely disgusted with them both. She passed away when I was nineteen. I've been on my own ever since."

She said it simply, a statement of fact. Taking control of her life ten years ago at such a young age had been hard, but she'd had to do it. It had been the right thing, she was sure.

TJ kissed her temple softly, then nestled her under his arm. He linked their fingers together and rested their joined hands in his lap. "Do you ever see your parents?"

She shook her head. "And it's not because I'm hiding from them. Honestly, I'm not bitter or wishing them ill anymore. I cut the ties and decided I was responsible for my own happiness. They just don't seem to give a damn. I think I remind them of each other or something, and they hate each other with a vengeance." She shrugged.

He grimaced. "So telling you stories about human happily-ever-afters..."

Pam leaned back on him and sighed. "Sheer fantasy. Werewolves are a whole lot more believable." A whole lot more desirable as well, from what she could tell. TJ appeared to know exactly who he was and where he stood.

Had he gained that confidence from being a wolf?

TJ stroked her fingers gently with his thumb. "I've had the pack around me all my life. While I get razzed a great deal for being clumsy, they've always supported me. My brother, my friends, heck...everyone."

"You're not clumsy."

He laughed out loud. "Okay, there's another topic for discussion. Umm, yes, I am. For some reason I'm not nearly as bad when I'm around you." He nuzzled her neck. "That 'you complete me' thing."

She slapped him lightly. "Get out. I think you're like a puppy coming into his growth. You should have seen the trouble my first dog had—"

He groaned. "Can we make a deal now that you don't compare me to your previous dogs. Please?"

A snort slipped out. "We'll see."

She twisted to stare at him. His earnest expression stole her heart.

"Pam, can you give me a clue here? Have I persuaded you at all what I said is true? That we're mates?"

Her fears and doubts scrambled to stay above the undeniable bond between them that grew stronger every moment she spent with him.

"Can't you tell what I'm thinking with that wolf connection of yours?" She couldn't speak over a whisper, the effort of pushing the words out enormous. She wanted to believe, wanted it so very much.

He surprised her by lifting her into his lap and tucking her head against his chest before setting the porch swing rocking. He surrounded her with his arms as if pulling a shield of protection around them. "I sense all kinds of things from you, and yet your emotions are so jumbled I can't understand. Fear, longing, sexual need. At times I feel as if you're about to announce you love me. The next minute you're planning to tell me goodbye and expect I'll drop you at the airport and let you go without a word of protest."

Umm, yup, that would about cover the gamut of chaos running through her brain the past couple days.

"Do you really pick up all those things, or are you guessing?"

It was his turn to sigh. "I can't literally read your mind, and we can't speak to each other mentally. But as far as I can tell, I'm just about as linked to you in terms of a mate connection as I could dream of."

"I feel like I've known you all my life." The whispered confession eased the tightness inside a little.

He squeezed her gently and kissed the top of her head. His heart thumped solidly under her ear, and she snuck her arms around his torso to draw as close as possible.

TJ sang to her *a capella*, his rich voice tickling her ears. Filling her with hope and a deep longing.

My love will never fade, it lingers like the light.
Fills all the mountaintops, burning ever bright.
My love is like the tide, fresh and clean each day.
It's pure and strong, and all that I can say—
You fill my days, you fill my nights, you're everything, all I need,
Forever
My love is like the spring, it lingers like the snow.
It only melts away, to bring new growth.
My love is like the wind, running wild and free.
Together now, won't you come with me—
You fill my days, you fill my nights, you're everything, all I need,
Forever

He let the words trail off, the intensity of his song wrapped up with all the things she felt from him. His tender heart. His humour. Plain spoken and blunt, but never cruel, he was all the things she admired in a friend. All the things she wanted in a lover.

Her final doubts dissolved. Logic had a place in this, and he'd done his best to show her the mate list existed and examples of each item. But at some point, the heart had to take over from the head and that moment was now.

She pressed her palm against his cheek and kissed him softly before crawling off his lap and holding out her hand.

"What—?"

She shook her head. One finger held to her lips, she poured her energy into sharing what she felt inside. The deep satisfaction at his company. The passion she held for him.

The love.

They walked together, hand in hand, into the cabin where she led him to the bedroom. She stripped off her clothes quickly and turned to help him. With every touch of her hands, she thought of a moment he'd made her smile the past week. Of an expression she'd seen on his face. Of the love she'd seen in his eyes. She didn't need any more words —he'd been saying it to her all week long with every gesture, every touch.

Every time he'd shifted into his wolf and wandered at her side, or curled up against her, soft and warm. He was completely comfortable in both his skins, and there was no deceit in him.

She tugged him to the bed and they connected, skin on skin, hands brushing, exploring. Their lips met in a breathless kiss that began soft and gentle before turning ravenous. Greedy and passionate, they rolled together until she managed to maneuver into position, his legs trapped under her. His cock breached the folds of her body and they slid together in one perfect moment. His breath released with a gasp and she felt his muscles tense as he realized they were making love without any barrier between them.

TJ gathered her in his arms and peered into her eyes. He didn't ask if she was sure, didn't do anything to break the beauty of her gift. He didn't even speak, not with words.

But his eyes said *I love you.*

His body said it. So did all the emotion she sensed from him, whether a figment of her imagination or not. All signs said he was hers, completely.

They moved together, hips rocking, tension building. The aching need to be filled by him, not only physically, but in every way, being answered. Kisses upon kisses fell while TJ's hands roamed her body. He slid into her again and again, drawing her thigh high over his hip as they lay side by side on the mattress. She teetered on the edge of release. He buried his face in her neck, rising slightly to press deeper into her core, the angle change pressing harder against her clit. The tickly sensation preceding her climax had never built this high before, and every nerve screamed for satisfaction. She had no idea how intense her body's response would be when he put his teeth to her neck and bit down, burying himself deep as they both went off together.

Bright white pleasure raced over her, every bit of skin sensitive and tingling. Every breath of air tasted like him, every thought wrapped up in his love. Their bodies meshed, intimate and close, as waves of bliss pulsed repeatedly. The bundle of dreams she'd tied up and put aside as impossible unwound.

Forever was not a myth, no more than werewolves.

They lay tangled together for the longest time, their breathing slowly returning to normal. TJ kissed her—her neck, her cheek, her forehead. One soft lingering kiss to her mouth.

He spoke, their lips brushing together. "I can feel your heart in my soul."

10

———

TJ closed the door to the cabin with reluctance. Neither of them was ready to leave.

He turned to see Pam grinning at him, her pack already on her back as they prepared to meet the helicopter. It still seemed impossible she'd taken that final step and accepted him. One day to celebrate being fully mated—it wasn't enough.

"I should have taken a two-week excursion. Then we could have stayed for another week."

She held out her hand and he joined her, strolling to the meadow with their fingers linked together.

TJ lifted her fingers to his mouth and kissed her knuckles lightly. "While I'd love more time alone, at some point we need to face the real world."

Oh hell, and there would be some facing to do. Funny though, now that he and Pam were fully mated, he wasn't nearly as worried to see what the fallout from his actions would be. They truly were together—there was no denying it—and no one could tear them apart.

They dropped their packs at the side of the clearing and Pam returned to his arms, resting her head on his chest. She drew a deep breath. "Can we come back here sometime?"

"Definitely."

He played with her hair as they silently stood together. Ever since they'd completed their mating, he had a solid line on what she was feeling. Compared to how it had been before, the richness and depth was incredible. Like having watched an old-fashioned black-and-white movie on a five-inch screen and now getting Blu-ray, hi-def flashing across a wall-sized monitor.

Right now she was content, and he was going to do everything he could to keep her that way.

"You know we've got a bunch of 'meet the family' to do, right?" he warned her.

Pam lifted her arms to drape them around his neck. "I think I can handle it. Maggie and Erik won't be back yet, but I'm not afraid to meet your brother, or his wife, more formally. Or anyone else I need to see."

TJ kissed her, unable to resist one more dose of her taste to bolster him. It was going to be an interesting day, if nothing else.

The sound of the chopper reached them long before they spotted it in the distance, and she clung to him for a second, squeezing him tight. "I know we've got a ton to figure out, but, honestly? It'll all work out. I'm sure it will."

"Of course it will." Her faith became his faith, and together, there was nothing they couldn't do.

Shaun landed, his grinning face peering out the window. They tossed their packs into the passenger area and scrambled after them, strapping themselves in and quickly donning headsets.

They lifted off, and Pam hung over him to gaze back at the cabin and lake as they swung around to return to Haines. Her body was warm and soft against him, and he wrapped an arm around her to keep her close.

"Well, I don't have to ask if you had a good time." Shaun's voice cut in over the headset. "Congratulations, both of you."

Pam glanced at TJ in surprise. He pressed the talk button to explain. "The wolf sense of smell. Shaun can tell we're mates."

"He can tell..." She flushed. "Okay, maybe I'm not so ready to meet your pack as I thought."

TJ grabbed her hand and squeezed.

Shaun spoke again. "I need to give you the scoop. I managed to stay off your big brother's radar for the past week, but I got a direct order from my Alpha in Whitehorse to report to him as soon as I get you two home safe. Which is fine, since that means I won't have to face Keil."

TJ swore. "I didn't intend to get you in trouble when I asked for help."

"Hey, no worries. You would have done the same thing for me if you could. You're a good friend, TJ, and it's nice to have been able to assist you two lovebirds. I don't think my Alpha will give me shit—he's a romantic at heart. Makes us watch bad chick flicks during pack meetings, yada yada."

"Still, let me know if you need me to come and talk to your Alpha. I have a feeling I'll be explaining myself constantly for the next while."

Shaun held a thumbs-up. "Anyway, I contacted your pack via email to let them know I'd drop you at the airstrip. Someone should be there to pick you up. I'm afraid you're on your own after that."

Pam's hand in his was all the reminder he needed. "I'm never going to be alone again."

She leaned against him and used the headset. "So, the shit is about to hit the fan, is it?"

"Don't know why it should. You're not going to call the cops and have me arrested, right?"

"I am the cops."

They grinned at each other.

A BEIGE MINIVAN stood at the side of the airstrip—Tad and Missy's vehicle—and TJ breathed a sigh of relief. The pack Omegas would be the perfect people to talk to first.

TJ passed down the packs to Pam then squeezed Shaun on the shoulder. "Thanks again for everything."

"Hey, give me a second." Shaun twisted in his seat to face TJ. "You know what? I think they're going to be very surprised when they meet you—your brother and the rest of them. You've changed. Something happened to you and you're more than the wolf I dropped off a week ago."

TJ frowned. "What do you mean?"

Shaun shook his head. "Not sure, but let's put it this way, I doubt I could order you to do anything for me anymore."

Fuck. "Really?"

"Really." Shaun winked at him and turned back to his instrument panel. "Now get out of here, your mate is waiting for you."

TJ joined Pam on the tarmac and they shouldered their packs, heading toward the van.

His mind spun. Shaun couldn't order him around? Shaun had always outranked him—heck most wolves seemed to outrank him. Not that they made a big deal of it, but usually he was "the younger brother of the Alpha" and otherwise not very interesting to most of the pack.

Tad stepped from the van and popped the hatch. Then he stood back and looked them up and down while they piled their backpacks into the vehicle. His wry smile was somewhat reassuring.

"Welcome back. And welcome to the pack, Pam. Congratulations on your mating."

Pam tugged on TJ's sleeve. "Everyone knows on sight we're together. This is going to take some serious getting used to."

TJ opened the passenger door for her and helped her in. "I said there were things that were hard to explain—you kind of have to experience them to understand." He scooted into the backseat.

She turned to answer Tad who had crawled behind the wheel. "Thanks. You'll have to warn me if I do something wrong. You're the pack...Omega, right?"

Tad nodded. "TJ explained a little about how wolves operate?"

"Yeah, he explained a lot. That doesn't mean much until I see it in motion. Bottom line, I didn't plan on joining any country clubs, I just..."

"We just want to be together." TJ eased forward between the seats, laying a hand on Pam's arm.

"Well, together is great and all that, but I hope you're ready to face the music. Robyn's been walking around all week like a thunderstorm ready to happen, and Keil got back half an hour ago and he's brewing up a storm as well. Missy is trying to settle them both down before we arrive, but we'll see how well it works."

"They'll have to get over it." The words were braver spoken than the pit in his stomach acknowledged.

Pam glanced over her shoulder and a breeze-like sensation brushed him. She pictured them sitting together, him making music, her admiring the scenery. She gave her calm to him and he pulled her fingers to his lips.

He kissed them softly then whispered, "Cool trick."

She grinned. "I think I'm getting the hang of this."

Tad hummed. "This is interesting. I can read you, TJ, like I normally can, but Pam—it's like she's wolf and yet not. I had no idea you were able to share emotions in a mating between humans and wolves."

"But you haven't been a full wolf for long, have you?" Pam asked.

"No. Still, at the core, what I do sense is that you two belong together, and you're good for each other. But that's my interpretation, and it's not my place to make decisions about your life for you."

"Damn straight," Pam muttered.

TJ laughed. "Speak up now, Pam, tell us how you really feel."

Tad smiled. "So, what *have* you decided?"

She dragged aside the collar of her T-shirt to reveal the mark TJ had left when he bit her. The wound had healed way faster than they'd expected—some kind of wolfie magic.

Tad nodded. "Well, that's pretty cut and dried. You know, it's kind of interesting not being able to read you the same way I can read the rest of the pack. I think you're going to be good for us all."

He turned down the long, narrow driveway that led to the cluster of homes built against the trees on the outskirts of Haines. He pulled up in front of an older log house, a wide veranda running the length of the building. TJ scrambled out to join Pam. A tricycle with pink streamers sat in the middle of the walkway, and Tad pushed it to the side as they approached the front doors.

TJ grasped Pam's hand in his, locking fingers.

"I feel like we should be offered a last meal or something." Pam hummed part of the funeral dirge, and TJ laughed.

Tad frowned at them. "What song was that?"

Pam rolled her eyes and glared at TJ. "See, I told you I couldn't sing. So much for your lessons that night at the cabin."

TJ shrugged. "I'm your mate, I'm not a miracle worker."

She growled and swung at him.

He caught the blow and pulled her against him, capturing her lips. She tasted like sunshine and sex, and if he didn't need to go see what Keil and Robyn had planned as retribution, he would pick her up and go hide in the woods for a few hours.

Or a few days. He was easy.

She kissed him back, her fingers lacing through his hair. He loved the way her tongue took control, exploring and teasing until all his body heard the wake-up call. She moved closer, her soft skin and strong muscles matching him perfectly. Especially when he reached down and cupped her butt, dragging her tighter against him and—

"TJ, Pam. So glad you could drop in." Keil's deep voice cut through the sexual fog and they wrenched apart. His brother spun on his heel and entered the house, leaving the door open behind him.

Pam's cheeks were flushed, but she lifted her chin high and stepped forward by his side.

"He's not really a jerk. I mean, sometimes he is, but usually he's a pretty good guy. Really." Although it appeared this might be one of the "jerk" days.

Pam snorted. "Don't worry about me, I have a feeling it's your ass he wants in a sling."

TJ nodded slowly. "Well, there is that."

They entered the main room and TJ counted heads. Keil and Robyn, Tad and Missy. A number of other high-level wolves were in attendance, but on the whole it seemed like a pretty friendly gathering.

Well, friendly except for Robyn, who gave him the evil eye as she leaned against the far wall. Keil stood at the foot of the staircase, arms crossed in front of his chest like a freaking bulldozer, ready to crush him underfoot.

Complete confidence held TJ up. Beside him stood his mate, her amusement at the situation flowing to him and calming his concerns. Heck, if she wasn't worried, why should he be? These were his family and friends. There was nothing they would do to him that wasn't done out of love.

"Umm, hi, everyone. You all met Pam at the wedding, but I'd like to introduce her again. It's official, she's accepted me as her mate."

Like that was a surprise to anyone with a nose, but he figured for Pam's sake he should say it, before some wiseass decided to ask how in the world they had managed to get as sex-scented as they were.

It wasn't his fault they took that final shower together. It had been all her idea.

Keil moved closer, towering over him. "Don't you ever pull such a harebrained stunt again. What the hell were you thinking?" he roared.

TJ opened his mouth to respond when Pam stepped between them. She pasted her fists on her hips and glared up at Keil. "Don't you shout at him. He's already apologized to me and I'm the only one he needs to worry about."

Holy shit. Keil's jaw nearly hit the floor.

Off to the side Tad stared at the ceiling, biting his lip. TJ watched closely. He could have sworn Tad was laughing.

Keil cleared his throat and glanced around the room sheepishly. When he spoke again, he turned down the volume and spoke more respectfully. "I'm sorry, you're right. There's no need for me to raise my voice. I'm not talking about you and him right now. I'm talking about him not leaving word of where he had arranged to take you, or having a backup plan to contact help if you got in trouble. He knows that's not proper procedure in terms of safety in the wilderness."

Pam nodded slowly. "Oh. I thought you were going to give him grief for kidnapping me. By all means, if he screwed up protocol—ream him out." She stepped back and gestured with a hand.

The room broke into laughter.

Keil raised a brow. "So kind of you to give me permission."

TJ scratched his face to hide his own smile. Yup, this was going to work out fine, once he took his lumps, because Keil was right about the safety issues.

Keil hauled a cell phone out of his pocket and slapped it into TJ's palm. "You'll probably need this—I found it back at base camp after you took off. Oh, and did you even *try* the satellite phone you took with you? The batteries on that one were nearly dead."

A solid smack landed on his arm as Pam hit him. "Dead? What if I'd wanted to call for the chopper?"

"But you broke…" TJ buttoned his lip. There was no way he was even going to touch this one.

Pam growled at him, her eyes flashing. "Next time, let me do the trip planning."

TJ tried to hide his smile. "Of course."

"Well, that's interesting. She's the most alpha human I've ever met," one of the observer wolves piped up.

Pam frowned. "Alpha? Isn't that your position?" she asked Keil.

He shook his head. "Yes and no. Alpha isn't just about leadership, it also refers to how strong you are, mentally as well as physically. There's more than one alpha wolf in any pack. Heck, Erik and Maggie, the pack Betas, are as strong as Robyn and I, but they've chosen to use their strengths in a different way. We can't all be bad-asses, you know."

"So there's no trouble with us being together?" Pam returned to TJ's side.

Keil shrugged. "There are a few old-timers in the pack who are whining about how the world is going to hell in a hand basket, but it's nothing I can't take care of."

Robyn clapped her hands and Keil pulled a face. "Oh yeah, and Robyn plans on having a long talk with your mate about some advice she gave that he ignored."

Oh shit. Okay, that was scarier than getting called on the carpet by Keil. TJ waved at Robyn tentatively and she flipped him the bird.

Pam grinned at TJ. "You know how I said I wasn't sure about dealing with your pack? No problem, I got it figured out. This is like hanging out at headquarters with the boys."

Tad stepped forward and gestured to the couch. "If you'd like to relax, I think the formal hazing is over. I do have one last question I'm curious about, and maybe someone with more experience can answer. What's up with TJ's strength? I'd swear he's gotten stronger since he left."

"Shaun said the same thing. What are you talking about? I don't feel any different." TJ sat next to Pam. She kicked off her shoes and curled up almost in his lap. She tucked a hand under his arm and tickled his ribs lightly. "The only thing I know is I don't seem to be nearly as clumsy anymore. Well, relatively speaking."

Tad's mate, Missy, paced the floor to sit on the second couch across from them, one of her two-month-old babies cuddled against her shoulder. "Your wolf never has been clumsy."

Pam leaned forward. "I think his wolf is more grown up. Matured a bit. If TJ is twenty-two, that means his wolf is…" She turned to face him and asked, "What are wolf years, seven like dogs?"

He groaned. "You promised you wouldn't do that anymore."

Pam smirked at him. "If you're gonna play with the big dogs, you use every tool you can."

He opened his mouth to protest, and suddenly the cell phone Keil had returned to him rang. Some joker had reprogrammed the phone tones to "Who Let the Dogs Out" and Pam cracked up.

He stood to answer it, leaving Pam and Missy giggling together furiously.

"Hello?"

"You idiot. You couldn't wait until we were done our honeymoon? *Sheesh.*"

"Hi, Maggie." TJ took a deep breath. So much for him being stronger. There was no way he could get a word in edgewise with all these women around. He listened to her scolding for a minute before he had the most brilliant idea. "Hey, Maggie. I bet you need to talk to Pam. She's right here."

He held out the phone to his mate and she took it. Her surprise turned to delight, and she rose to find a quieter spot to chat with her best friend.

TJ glanced around the room. Missy rocked one baby in her arms while Tad paced with her twin sister. Robyn was holding a conversation with someone, her hands moving rapidly.

Kara, Keil and Robyn's two-year-old daughter, crossed the room to Pam's side. She tugged on Pam's pant leg then reached her arms up.

Pam leaned over and picked up the little girl who immediately wrapped herself close, her face buried in Pam's neck. Pam resumed her phone conversation.

Deep satisfaction filled TJ as everywhere he looked he saw family. Sharing together, laughing together. Little Jamie, Missy and Tad's oldest child, rolled on the floor with a couple of the pack in their wolf forms.

It wasn't the Waltons, but it was home.

He glanced back at Pam to find her staring at him, a burning light in her eyes. She adjusted the girl in her arms and waggled her brows, tilting her head toward the child.

Oh shit. Oh shit, yeah. Well, maybe not this minute, but…

TJ winked at her and she grinned, blowing him a kiss.

Keil poked him in the shoulder. "You haven't heard a word I've said, have you? What's that goofy expression for?"

TJ took a deep breath. His head filled with the familiar scents of home, and overlaying it all was Pam. In his head, and his heart.

Forever.

"It's because I'm finally in the right place, at the right time. Excuse me, I'll be back for my lickings regarding safety, because you're right, I screwed up. And I'll apologize to Robyn in a minute as well. But there's something I need to do with my mate."

He stepped across the room and tugged Pam into the kitchen, taking little Kara along for the ride since she refused to let go of her newfound friend. He held out his hand for the phone.

"Mags? I gotta go. I think TJ wants me to take him for a walk."

TJ rubbed his forehead as she said goodbye to Maggie. A dog handler. She must have a million jokes all lined up and ready to spring on him.

Pam handed back his cell and batted her eyes. "Well. I thought that all went marvelously."

He groaned. "Yeah, I can see this relationship is going to keep me on my toes. I wanted to know if you still had the mate list."

Pam frowned. "It's in my pocket. Why?"

"I never got to finish it."

She kissed Kara on the forehead then passed her to TJ. The little girl squirmed to be put down, returning with a laugh to the main room.

Pam reached into her back pocket and unfolded the paper on the counter. The edges were a little more tattered and ragged than when they'd started less than a week ago.

She cupped his face in her hands. "You proved enough for me to take a chance, and while we've still got stuff to figure out, I think we're on our way."

TJ grabbed a pen. "I agree, but there's something I need you to see. It's important."

There where the five circles overlapped, an empty space remained. He'd deliberately made sure it was a part of every single circle, and with great care he filled in one word.

Forever.

Pam sucked in air and threw her arms around his neck.

He stumbled for a second to catch his balance as she crawled up him and kissed him madly. Oh yes, she was going to fit in fine. A room full of people on the other side of the wall and she was happily attempting to touch his tonsils.

He clasped her under the hips and turned to carry her to one of the back guestrooms. No one would notice if they were MIA for an hour or so, would they?

"Stop," she ordered.

Shit. Please don't get all human shy. "They're all wolves. They wouldn't care if we had sex in the room in front of them."

Pam snorted. "Yeah, well, I doubt I'll ever get to that stage of comfort, but just let me get..." She leaned over and snatched the mate list off the counter. "Okay, now we can go fool around."

TJ laughed as he headed down the hall. "You keeping that list?"

"Uh-huh. Just like you wrote. I plan on keeping it, and you, forever."

BONUS SCENE

While they were working on the mate list, TJ gave Pam an impromptu singing lesson, and I've always wanted to share the scene but there wasn't room in the original novella. Here for you in this special Northern Lights Edition *is what happened that evening.*

~

TJ gave a final stir to two cups of hot chocolate and Bailey's while plotting furiously.

While he thought his "explain everything about mates to a person who didn't really understand wolves in the first place" adventure was going okay, it was impossible to be absolutely sure. He couldn't tell by Pam's reactions as she was keeping parts of herself pretty guarded, but there were hints that he wasn't doing too poorly. He still had three days, so spending a ton of time overanalyzing wasn't what he needed.

Instead, he placed one cup beside her before dropping to the floor, close enough that their thighs touched. She'd added another log to the fire, and the stove was crackling nicely, a beautiful, peaceful, *romantic* backdrop for their evening.

Pam curled her fingers around the cup and offered him a smile, and his heart went pitter patter all over again. "Thank you. That's so sweet."

Irresistible. "So are you." He waggled his brows, leaning in and pressing their lips together for a brief moment. He'd like to forget the flipping hot chocolate and just kiss her over and over again.

It would be too easy to keep going. To take the cup from her fingers, place it on the coffee table beside them, then haul her down to her back. To kiss along her jaw as he settled between her legs and…

Damn it, he hadn't just been thinking about it, he'd done it. Bodies close, rolling together with his erection pressed to her thigh.

She made a low moaning noise, and fire flew through his veins.

But this wasn't just about sex. It was about so much more, so he reluctantly pulled back, forcing them both to vertical.

Although it was very nice to see the same heat in her eyes as he stared into her face. "We'll pick that up later," he promised. "Right now we have some lessons to work through, young lady."

Pam nodded slowly, dragging herself back to that fine-tuned and steely concentration he was sure helped her a ton when it came to her job.

She took a sip of the hot chocolate, her eyes widening. "Whoa. That's going to pack a punch."

"Not enough to get drunk," he said.

"What if I want to get tipsy?"

He shook his head. "You need to be in full possession of your wits at all times this week." He said it teasingly, but firmly like the absolute truth it was.

She nodded, taking another sip before putting the cup away carefully. "Agreed, it's why I will sally-forth into the singing lesson, while barely making mention of the irony of *you* calling me 'young lady'." She cupped his face with a hand. "I am such a cradle robber."

He caught her hand before she could steal away the heat of her palm. That momentary touch shot more adrenaline into him than any shot of espresso. "We wolves mature far faster than humans," he informed her.

"Oh, like dog years?"

He kept a straight face. "Something like that."

She smirked but stayed silent.

He sat back slightly. "You ever watched The Sound of Music?"

She tilted her head to one side and gave him a *are you crazy?* look.

Enough said. "Let's start with a little run through on the 'Doe, a deer' thing."

Pam shrugged. "It's your eardrums."

"I'm sure you're not that bad."

But by the time they'd reached "Ray", he'd been proven far too optimistic. Rarely could she find a note in the first place, and whatever she did hit, she couldn't hold. As they carried on, he did his best to give no sign of the pain she was inflicting on him.

Surprisingly, it was clear she had no idea *how* bad she was. Oh, she'd warned him she didn't know how to sing, but she was enthusiastic, increasing in confidence and volume—dear lord, have mercy—the farther she got into the song.

But even with over-the-top enthusiasm, she couldn't have sung her way out of a paper bag. If she had to sing for her supper she would've starved within a week. And that was being generous.

TJ was suddenly struck with a dilemma. If this had been anybody else in the pack who had wanted singing lessons, like say his friend, Mark Weaver, at this point in the game TJ would have shut down the lessons in order to save his sanity. No hesitation. Because Mark was never going to be a singer, and in some ways it was better if he didn't even try.

But Mark also didn't really give shit. The guy was laid-back enough that he could use his disadvantage to an advantage as comedy relief, or he would simply move on to something else, or get distracted, which he seemed to do a lot. Mark was a decent guy, but he had a lot on his plate.

Pam *loved* to sing. It was clear even as she protested and laid the groundwork to warn the people around her, she *wished* she could.

And she did sing. She just sang—poorly.

So as her mate he was damn well going to teach her how. Even though "Sew, a needle pulling thread" felt as if a spear was going in one ear, through his brain and out the other, taking part of his hearing system with it—he was going to teach her, or die in the attempt.

Anyone who made her feel bad about her talents in the future would have to deal with him.

His wolf stretched and agreed, testing its claws and teeth in preparation to protect. *Anything for our mate.*

The entire time TJ'd been thinking, they'd carried on...okay, he'd just call it *singing* to make it easier. But they were done now, and he had to figure out the next step because his original idea wasn't going to work.

"And there we go," Pam said with a bright smile, "I warned you."

He caught her fingers and squeezed. "You're not the worst singer I've ever heard."

She gasped. "Oh my God, that poor person."

A laugh burst from him. "Okay, I think that came out the wrong way, but don't worry about it. Instead, think about this..."

TJ pressed a kiss to her palm. She hummed happily in response. A nice smooth middle F, if his ears weren't wrong. Oh yeah, this was going to work.

He kissed her hand again then slid farther north, flicking his tongue against her skin all the way up to her elbow.

The hum in F turned into a long moan in G.

He stopped and played at the inside of her elbow, smiling against her skin because the noises she made when he touched her there were a deeper kind of F *hmmm* with little bits of A and high C *oooooh* in between each of them. Excitement heightened like an eager drum roll through him.

He pulled back and checked her face. She was breathing hard, cheeks flushed, her eyes half-lidded. "I have no idea what you're doing," she told him, "but I like it."

"So do I."

He pushed her back to the rug, pulling over top of her. His weight rested on his elbows so that their bodies barely touched. She groaned, this time higher pitched, like a question. She'd slipped up an octave.

He placed his face in the crook of her neck, and his wolf went wild for a moment before the beast settled down and helped TJ concentrate. He licked, and kissed, and licked some more. Nibbling at her earlobe until she was purring (B flat).

She dragged her fingers through his hair as he slipped down her body, plumping her breast, dragging his teeth across the erect nipple behind her shirt. Farther down, farther down, as a series of sounds followed him. He dragged off her sweatpants and dropped between her thighs.

That's when the song really took off. Every lick, every caress, every time he touched her another sigh of delight escaped, and *here* was a beautiful melody. A symphony echoing off the walls of the small cabin like the joyful noise he needed to hear, and when she finally sang out her orgasm, he didn't bother to try and hide his smile. Just curled his lips against her belly before shifting northward to settle at her side.

Pam dragged her hands through his hair again and again, and his wolf damn near smirked.

"Whoa, that was a lot of fun," she let out on a happy sigh.

TJ levered himself back beside her. "You sang great."

She hesitated. "I don't know what you're talking about."

"The song you just sang. Totally awesome."

A laugh burst from her.

"Sing something for me," he ordered.

She rolled her eyes good-naturedly before placing her hands behind her head and diving into a tune.

"Do you want—?" He cupped her breast, and the words escaping her slid from out of tune into this breathless, gorgeous note. Her eyes widened. "Seriously?"

TJ shrugged. "It worked. And admit it—the lesson was pretty fun."

"Wait until the next time somebody wants me to do karaoke. You have to come up with me, and they'll end up with a porno show at the same time."

Not going to happen anytime soon because he wasn't ready to have anyone else see her O face. "Are you ready for a more advanced lesson?"

He pulled her to her feet so the fronts of their bodies rubbed. She caught him by the hand and whirled him into a dance around the living room, one that somehow finished with them mysteriously tumbling into bed. "Oh look at that. I have no idea how it happened."

TJ laughed. "Perfect. The acoustics in here are even better than the other room."

Pam snickered. "I still can't sing," she reminded him.

He shook his head, nuzzling against her affectionately and making sure the truth in his words was crystal clear. "Your singing makes you happy, which makes me happy, and that's all that's necessary. Got that? Anytime, anywhere, I will sing with you."

Her eyes sparkled like stars in the sky. "Thank you."

TJ nodded firmly, and when she brushed her hands over his back and attempted to pull him down for a kiss, he made her wait. He reached over his head and dragged off his shirt before doing the same to her, then settled happily into her embrace. "Lesson number two starts now..."

EPILOGUE

Two years later, June, Haines Alaska

Jared Gilliland loved his life. Because, what was there not to love? He had a great pack to belong to, friends to help and to get into mischief with, and—

"Oh sweet heaven above the angels in glory and whoa and damn and I hear bells am I supposed to hear bells?" A soft, breathless nonsense phrase delivered in a light soprano from the young woman lying naked, collapsed limply on the mattress beside Jared.

They'd just finished enjoying some rather vigorous exertions, and her legs twitched against his thigh as she let out a mighty sigh.

He rolled to his side to stare down at her in amusement. "Happy?"

She didn't open her eyes. "Don't know. Can't talk. Can't think. You killed me."

Jared laughed. "Don't be dead. Considering it's only eight o'clock, it would put a damper on our fun as I am *not* into necrophilia."

Her lips curled a smile. "Holy moly, Jared, that was amazing."

"Thank you, I know."

"I'd poke you about having an ego, but it ain't bragging if you done it." Another sigh of contentment escaped her.

"I'll be right back," he promised, kissing the tip of her nose before rolling out of bed and heading naked for the kitchen.

He took his time, strolling slowly and checking out her apartment as he went—may as well give her a few minutes to recover.

She had a nice place. Neat, lots of comfy furniture with walls lined with bookcases full of knickknacks, books, and framed pictures with a lot of family and friends.

He stuck his head in the fridge and got them a couple of drinks, carrying them back to her bedroom.

The blonde had managed to pull herself to a sitting position, her sex-tousled hair and bright smile making her look mighty tasty. She reached out her hand eagerly for the glass he carried. "Oh, thank you."

They downed the drinks, chatting for a bit. Laughter and teasing easy between them.

She leaned back on a pillow, suddenly more serious. "I hate to change the topic, but you do remember I'm not looking for a serious relationship right now."

Jared nodded. "So you said. Me too—just fun."

"Fun, and lots of orgasms." A jaunty wink.

"Naturally, lots of those." Jared tipped a finger under her chin. "No problem, babe. You mentioned that earlier when we met. I'm not going to get growly on you."

She dipped her head firmly. "I'm glad. It's just nice to not have to do the 'meet the family' thing every time, and have all these expectations, and wondering about where things are going. I just want to enjoy your company for a while."

Jared was doubly glad. Doing a meet and greet with his family was *not* on the agenda—a total logistical nightmare for so many reasons. And the fact he was a wolf shifter and she wasn't just added to the 'this is not a long term relationship' situation.

Not that he was totally opposed to the idea of finding a long-term. Heck, even his friend TJ had found his mate, which a month ago had to have been like a *two out of ten* on the scale of things most likely to happen.

Still, it *had* happened, and Jared was glad for his friend. But lightning rarely struck twice: the odds of Jared ever finding a mate were probably a million to one.

He shoved off his momentary gloom and slid a finger down her arm, watching as she squirmed. "Are you ready to enjoy my company a little more right now? Because I have this itch I need to scratch."

She put aside her glass and reached for him, and the evening's entertainment moved to the next stage. If he couldn't have a mate, he could at least have a damn good time. Jared pushed aside the things he couldn't control and worked the things he could.

Life was good. As good as it was going to get. And that was fine with him.

Inside, though, his wolf folded its tail under and pouted. *Silly human.*

The human side could lie all he wanted, but his wolf knew better. Fun was fun, he supposed, but a mate was more than fun.

Something was missing, and the beast wasn't going to give up until he'd found her.

Mate. She's out there...

~

New York Times Bestselling Author Vivian Arend
brings you a series of light-hearted,
stand-alone novellas, with fated mates and always a
happily-ever-after.

~

Granite Lake Wolves
Wolf Signs
Wolf Flight
Wolf Games
Wolf Tracks
Wolf Line
Wolf Nip

~

ABOUT THE AUTHOR

With over 2 million books sold, Vivian Arend is a New York Times and USA Today bestselling author of over 50 contemporary and paranormal romance books, including the Six Pack Ranch and Granite Lake Wolves.

Her books are all standalone reads with no cliffhangers. They're humorous yet emotional, with sexy-times and happily-ever-afters. Vivian pretty much thinks she's got the best job in the world, and she's looking forward to giving readers more HEAs. She lives in B.C. Canada with her husband of many years and a fluffy attack Shih-tzu named Luna who ignores everyone except when treats are deployed.

www.vivianarend.com